DEMON ESCAPE

THE RESURRECTION CHRONICLES

M.J. HAAG

DEMON ESCAPE

Copyright: M.J. Haag

Published: February 27, 2018

ISBN-13: 978-1-985073-73-9

Cover Design: Shattered Glass Publishing LLC

Series Reading Order

By M.J. Haag and Becca Vincenza

Demon Ember

Demon Flames

Demon Ash

By M.J. Haag

Demon Escape

To my readers who continue to support my work with each purchase,

Thank you and here's another one!

DEMON ESCAPE

Eden Terry survived the first ring of hell only to end up in the second one.

With nothing but a trowel and her wits, she's determined to escape the work camp holding her prisoner. She dreams of finding a safe haven and living in the new, devastated world on her own.

However, surviving alone after she escapes proves more difficult than she ever imagines. While running from zombies and hellhounds, a new creature emerges. This one isn't after her blood. He wants much more.

Eden must decide who the real devils are between man and demon. Choosing wrong could cost her life; choosing correctly could lead her to the haven she's been searching for.

What has happened before...

Weeks ago, earthquakes unleashed hellhounds on an unsuspecting mankind. The bite of a hound changes humans, turning people into flesh-eating infected.

The hellhounds weren't the only thing to emerge from the earthen caverns. Demon men with grey skin and reptilian eyes have been trapped underground for thousands of years. They alone can kill the hellhounds and help bring a stop to the plague. They only ask for one thing in return: a chance to meet women who might be willing to love them as they are.

One

I clawed my fingers into the dirt.

"Eden, what are you doing?" a male voice said from right behind me.

"Digging for carrots, asshole; what do you think?"

"Aw, don't talk like that. There are so many nicer things a pretty girl like you should do with your mouth instead."

"Yeah, like bite your dick off." I pulled a carrot from the cold, hard ground and threw it over my shoulder.

Van chuckled, and I knew he'd caught it.

"Good find, Eden. This is why you're our favorite."

I said nothing. Instead, I crab walked forward, looking for the wilted remains of another carrot top.

"You know you don't need to be out here," he said. "You could be warm and comfortable back at the bunker."

"No thanks."

I used my trowel to scrape away the dead weeds, then my fingers to dig up the carrot. Using my fingers meant an undamaged root and more food. It also meant my hands were numb already. I tossed the new find over my shoulder, too.

"One of these days, you'll change your mind," he said. "And, I bet it'll be sooner than you think."

I listened to Van's steps as he walked away, and I tried to

quell the dread consuming my stomach. What did he mean sooner than I thought? What did he have planned?

Turning my head, I watched him walk toward the work truck where four of the other gunmen kept an eye on the eight of us. My fellow workers, who were also looking for missed carrots in the abandoned field, didn't bother to look at our protectors. Most of their attention wasn't on the ground but on the trees around us.

At the first sign of an infected, they would scramble back to the truck and likely run right into the line of fire. I'd seen two workers die that way already in the two weeks I'd been here. It seemed like a lifetime ago, though. How many weeks had it been since the quakes had caused everything to go to shit?

"Keep digging," one of the men in the truck said. I couldn't be sure which of the men was speaking, but I got back to work anyway. I didn't want to draw unwanted attention.

We worked for another hour as the sun passed its zenith.

"Back to the truck." Van nudged my shoulder with the point of his rifle to punctuate his words.

I picked up my basket of carrots and headed toward the truck. When I reached it, I waited in line as Van collected what we'd found. Like most of the gunmen, he looked cleaner than the workers. Non-greasy blonde hair, baby-blue eyes, and a classically handsome face didn't make him appealing, though.

"Were you even digging?" he said to the first person. I didn't look to see who he spoke to but kept my eyes on the ground.

Van moved down the line, muttering complaints about the lack of food each person had found. What did he expect? We'd picked over this field three times already, and that was after the field had already been harvested at the end of the growing season...before the hellhounds started turning people into flesh-eating infected.

"Eden, look at you," Van said, stopping in front of me. "This is what I'm talking about, people. There's a full two dozen carrots here. Pat them down. Anyone stealing loses tonight's ration." His fingers touched my chin, forcing my gaze up to meet his. "What about you, Eden? Trying to steal?"

"What do you think?" We both knew I wouldn't dream of trying to keep something for myself. Just like we both knew that didn't really matter.

"Oh, sugar, I think I need to check." He took the basket from my hands and passed it off to one of the grinning idiots behind him. Then he unzipped my jacket and groped me under the pretext of a carrot search.

After a minute, I wacked the back of his hand with my trowel.

"If you can't tell the difference between a breast and a carrot by now, maybe I should be the one with the gun."

He grinned at me as he shook out his hand.

"I think you're safer with your little shovel. Get in back."

I wasn't safer with my trowel. He was.

I crowded into the bed of the pickup with the rest of the workers and hung onto the sides. The truck rumbled to life and quickly bumped its way out of the field at higher speeds than safe for those in the back. Unlike most every other action carried out by our armed guards, they weren't driving fast to be dicks. We all knew the sound of the engine would draw the infected if we stayed in one place too long.

The truck cleared the fields and turned onto the road that led back to the bunker. Van's smirking gaze kept returning to me the closer we got to home, and a sinking feeling consumed my insides. He had something planned, and I doubted it would be anything that benefited me.

I huddled further into my winter jacket and wished I still had a hat. My long brown hair didn't keep my head warm or shelter my ears from the biting wind. All I could do to brace against the cold was tuck my hands into the armpits of my coat and wait for the ride to be over.

As soon as the truck stopped, everyone began to pile out and shuffle toward the reinforced steel door that led down to the bunker. I waited for my turn to get out, hating that I was back here.

Every time we left this place, I promised myself I would run once we reached the fields. I knew I was somewhere south of my home in Homer, Oklahoma; but didn't know exactly how far away I was, other than it being more than I could walk in a day. Not that it mattered. There was nothing left for me there anyway. With all the infected I'd seen when my parents and I had left, I knew I didn't want to go north when I ran. Heading east or west would be better. I'd definitely bypass all towns. A lot of buildings in one place meant a lot of infected, and I was smart enough to know what to avoid.

Yet, the guarantee of a cooked meal and of protection against hounds and infected kept me coming back. That, and the threat of being shot in the back if the guards caught me trying to run.

Van stood at the back of the truck and watched me hop down.

"Looks like you're about due for a shower. I'd be willing to partner up with you."

"I'd rather drink the water than waste it on washing. Besides, I'll just get dirty again tomorrow." I didn't pause on my way to the door. Van fell in step beside me.

"You sure? I hear it's half ration tonight. I'd be willing to give you my share."

That he was willing to entice me with food and go hungry to get me alone in the shower made my stomach clench worse.

"If you pass out because you didn't eat, we're all at risk. I'll stick to my own food."

I walked down the steps and wondered if I'd find myself washing backs like May tonight, regardless of my carefully worded protest.

Through the secondary hatch, the warmth of the bunker surrounded me along with the stink of chickens. Everyone moved toward the kitchen area. Only six could eat at a time. I didn't care that I was last. They kept the portions equal for those who worked in the fields. One scoop each of whatever Oscar cooked up. It smelled like beans and eggs again. Weeks ago, I would have laughed if someone had told me I'd scarf down that combination and wish for seconds.

At the front of the line, Grady started down the list of assigned duties for the night. It was the usual "clean the composting toilet, wash the dishes, guard the door" crap it was every night. Until he got to my name.

"The pen needs cleaning. Wait until everyone's done with dinner."

"The chicken pen? It hasn't been cleaned since I got here."

"Exactly. Our eyes will start burning if we don't get rid of the old straw and put down new. Are you gonna have a problem doing your job?"

Only one answer would get me dinner.

"No."

He shook his head like he was disappointed in me, like I was the problem, then moved on. Beyond him, I caught Van's smirk. Was this how he thought he'd get me in bed with him? Offer to take over a shit job, literally, in exchange for a little false affection later. No thanks. I'd pick shoveling shit any day.

It didn't take long to receive my ration of food and sit at the table. No one lingered over an empty plate. Sit. Eat. Leave. Staying only made a person wish there was more to eat, and seconds were never an option, no matter how many canned and dried goods lined the shelves of the enormous storage room.

Plate scraped clean, I set it in the sink and went to the back where we housed the chickens. The UV light hummed overhead, a background noise to the constant sounds of bird protest. Not that I blamed them. I didn't like being stuck underground either. However, the chickens appeared to be faring much worse. Their backs were almost clear of feathers.

I grabbed the pitch fork and opened the dog pen. It didn't take me long to clean away the old straw or lay down the new. Grabbing two of the five-gallon buckets I'd filled, I started toward the exit.

Van was already waiting for me. He opened the door and led the way to the top of the stairs. After he made sure it was clear, he opened the outer door and stood guard while I emptied the buckets into a compost heap nearby.

It would take three trips to remove all the used straw, and the sun wasn't getting any higher. So, I hurried back toward Van and started down the steps for the next trip.

No one spoke to me as I worked, which was just fine. It let me think about the past. About a time when being a pretty girl with green eyes and straight brown hair had been a good thing.

I'd grown up in the country with the unconditional love of my parents and our dog, Tam-Tam. I'd lost her first, the night the hellhounds came. My parents had been smart enough to hole up in our house instead of trying to run somewhere. We'd lasted the first week like that. Lights on at night to keep the hellhounds away, and doors locked during the day to keep the infected out.

Hearing distant explosions as nearby cities were bombed to hell had freaked my mom out, though. We should have stayed in our house. We shouldn't have tried to find somewhere safer. There wasn't anywhere safe left.

I dumped the second load onto the pile and turned back for the final load. Van watched me closely.

My parents and I had thought we would only need to worry about infected and hellhounds. However, with those bombs, the world had turned into "every man for himself." The first group of raiders to pick us up just outside of Roff had forced us to help with supply runs. They'd send us without weapons into houses to scavenge for supplies.

The infected had begun to grow smarter by then. Most of the traps they'd set had been easy to spot and avoid. A car moved to block the center of the road. A trail of food leading to a house. In the houses, though, the traps were different. It wasn't an object out of place but what waited in the shadows. The infected would hide in rooms and watch us as we passed, waiting for the right moment to take us unaware. I'd learned to defend myself with whatever was close at hand. Usually knives from abandoned kitchens. A few times, we found guns too. Need was the best teacher. I discovered how to shoot when needed and to make each bullet count because the noise drew more infected.

Mom had been the first to be bitten. Dad had managed to kill the infected with the leg of a broken chair before it could get either of us. I'd watched as he'd cried over Mom while she puked and stopped breathing. And, I'd watched as a part of him had died when she'd opened her eyes again.

Killing Mom had broken Dad, and he hadn't lasted much longer after that.

The hollow sound of the door shutting behind me brought me back to the present. I turned to look for Van but found myself alone outside the bunker.

Angry, I left the buckets and marched over to the door. Through the clear portal, I saw Van waiting for me. His muffled voice barely reached my ears.

"You want back in? You'll need to give me something for it."

"Stop messing around."

"You're starting to hurt my feelings, Eden. I'm not looking for some quick fuck. I've liked you since the moment we found you."

More like stole me.

"Why do you keep trying to put me off? We'll be good together. You'll see."

So, this was what he'd meant by sooner than I thought. I wasn't some virgin afraid of sex. Before everything had happened, I'd had several decent boyfriends who treated me like I was someone special. A far stretch from how Van wanted to treat me. And I refused to be his whore.

The sun was sinking lower. The wind rattled tree branches, but that was the only noise. No animals. No birds. I hated that about the new world. Everything silent like a lull before a shit storm. I glanced at the trees surrounding the place. They could be full of infected, just waiting. I wouldn't stand a chance without a weapon.

Van's steady blue gaze met mine. He knew exactly what I was thinking, and that's why he'd waited until the final trip to shut the door on me.

"A hand job. That's all," I said.

He grinned and released the lock.

"Once you put your hand on my cock, you won't be able to let go."

I wanted to punch the smirk off his face. Instead, I used my words as I slid past him and started down the stairs.

"In your dreams."

I only made it a step before he grabbed my hair. I squeaked and missed a step. His hold almost ripped hair from my scalp before I righted myself.

"Where do you think you're going? A deal's a deal, and I'm done being patient with you."

So was I. I swallowed my anger and kept my tone even.

"I figured you'd want to be further away from the door when the sun sets. After all, you said I wouldn't want to let go."

"You always have an answer, don't you?" He pulled me back against his chest then released my hair to grab my breast through my jacket. The next words he uttered were spoken against the side of my head.

"Lead the way, Eden." His tongue dragged against the shell of my ear, and I shuddered in disgust.

He took it as something else, though, because he moaned appreciatively and ground himself against my ass.

"I'll go slow with you," he promised before he released me.

I descended the steps with shaky legs and a stinging scalp. At the bottom, I waited for him to close the door. As soon as it was secure for the night, I reached for the waistband of his pants and slid my hand in.

"My hand is cold. Let me warm it up." I slowly brushed my palm against his raging boner while staring right into his eyes.

He hissed.

"Damn. It is cold."

"Don't worry. You'll appreciate it more in a second." When I reached the bottom of his shaft, I went straight for his balls.

There was a slight delay between squeezing the shit out of his testicles and his reaction. Once the "oh-fuck" signal reached his brain, his eyes widened and his mouth opened a bit to emit a low groan, not unlike the sound an infected would make.

"What is more important to you?" I asked. "Food or a fuck? Because I'm the only one here who seems to know her elbow from her ass when it comes to finding vegetables; and I can promise you, I will not be your worker and your whore. So choose."

Van's knees started to give out, but I didn't loosen my hold, just like he hadn't released my hair.

"Food's more important, Eden," Oscar said from behind me.

"Then tell your son that."

"I will. Now, let him go before you permanently damage him."

Oscar had always been the level-headed one of the bunch. I released my death grip on Van's scrotum and yanked my hand from his pants. The man slowly fell to his knees and hunched forward.

"Eden, you'll take the bunk next to mine tonight," Oscar said. "Go."

Van groaned behind me as I walked away.

"Your days are numbered, Eden," he managed to rasp.

I didn't stop to look back at him.

"It's the end of the fucking world. Of course they're numbered."

Two

After Van regained his ability to walk, he slunk off to his bed where he sat and glared at me for the remainder of the evening. An activity he continued as soon as he woken up this morning. I wasn't stupid. I'd only survived the night untouched thanks to Oscar's close proximity.

Ignoring Van, I stood in line for breakfast. More beans with eggs. However, when I stepped up to Oscar, he shook his head.

"You attacked one of the men. No rations for you today."

I couldn't believe my ears.

"He locked me outside and told me the only way to get back in was to sleep with him. Then, he grabbed me by the hair. So, intent to rape is okay and self-defense isn't? Is that what you're telling me?"

"We have a peaceful system that works. I'm telling you not to rock the boat. If there's a problem, you come to me. You don't handle it yourself."

"Wait until you're raped to report it. Got it." I set my plate aside and turned away.

May gave me a pitying look but didn't offer to share her ration. I wouldn't have accepted anyway. She put up with a lot for a few extra bites of food.

"Are we going to have problems with you, Eden?" Oscar asked after me.

"No, sir."

Because I didn't plan to stick around long. He and his son had finally given me the motivation I needed to commit to a plan to break out of their hell.

While the rest quickly ate, I stood by the inner hatch and plotted. I needed rations, water, and some kind of weapon. Rations would be hard to get. Granted, there was enough in the supply cage to last five months if they continued rationing and more than enough for me to choose from. But, Oscar guarded the key and took inventory every time he went in there.

Van, his rifle already slung over his shoulder, walked over and interrupted my thoughts.

"Maybe next time you'll be smarter," he said.

"Oh, I will be. I'm betting you won't though."

"Van! Keep away from Eden. Grady, go keep an eye on things."

Grady unlocked the hatch while Van continued to stare at me. I didn't look away. I refused to show fear or weakness.

"Come on, Van. You can help me clear the truck. Stay here, Eden."

Less than ten minutes later, the gunmen were in the cab, and the workers were in the back of the truck as it rumbled away from the bunker. I clutched my trowel and tried to ignore my growling stomach during the ride to the co-op field.

This far away from the cities, we didn't often see large groups of infected, so the ride to the field went quickly. Once the driver cut the engine, we stood and started getting out.

Grady handed me a basket when I had my feet on the ground.

"We want twice as much from you as yesterday, Eden. We need proof that you're worth the trouble you're causing."

"Worth the trouble I cause?" I snorted, took the basket, and started toward the field.

This field had a little of everything in it and wasn't as picked over because it had been community run. If I went closer to the trees, it wouldn't be too hard to find twice as many vegetables as the day before.

"This is our last chance to get as much fresh produce as we can, people. We're holing up for the winter after today. Make it count."

My feet faltered at his words. This was it? This was my last chance to escape, and I had nothing but my trowel with me?

"Problem, Eden?" Van said from nearby.

"Yeah, I just realized I need to go closer to the trees in order to find enough to make up for the shit you pulled yesterday. Thanks for nothing."

He chuckled behind me, and I kept moving forward. When I figured I'd walked halfway between the trucks and the trees, I stopped and looked back. Van wasn't far from me. However, he watched the trees instead of me now.

If only I had his gun and his bag of shells. I'd have a fighting chance, then.

I squatted down and started my search for vegetables while my mind raced. I dug, put my finding in the basket, then moved forward on autopilot. There had to be a way for me to overpower him like I did yesterday. I doubted he'd let me near his junk again, though.

"That's far enough." Van's softly spoken warning made me grin with inspiration.

"There's a ton of stuff over here. Look at my basket." I moved forward and dug a beet out of the ground.

"It's not worth getting killed."

"You have a gun; and unless there's a hound in there, we can outrun anything that might try for us. Besides, I forgot to pee before we left, and I'm not going to pee on our food source. You can keep an eye on me when I go into the trees."

"Not happening."

I stood and faced him.

"I thought you wanted to see me bare-assed."

I smothered my grin as he reached for the radio in his pocket.

"Eden's gotta pee. We're stepping into the trees. It might take a few minutes once she has her pants down."

Grady answered.

"Your old man's going to be pissed if you try anything again. Just hurry up."

Van nodded for me to get going into the trees. Heart hammering, I walked toward their shadowy depths. I was taking a huge risk, but I needed that gun.

Leaves crunched under each carefully placed step. When I found a big tree, I looked at Van with wide eyes that I didn't need to fake then scanned the area. Neither of us spoke.

I motioned to myself then the tree. He glanced back at the field and the truck, which were still visible. I needed to get him out of sight.

My hands shook as I stepped behind the tree and slowly pulled down my zipper. Like a fly drawn to honey, Van shuffled forward so he could see me. Instead of dropping my pants, I spread my feet apart, stuck my left hand into my underwear, and pretended to play with myself.

Van swore softly.

"I knew it," he whispered.

He moved closer. I parted my lips and closed my eyes,

giving my best impression of a girl about to quietly come. His palm covered my breast, and his lips touched mine.

Gripping the handle of my trowel, I lifted my right hand and hit him with the blunt end. I missed the top of his head, like I'd aimed, and clipped him hard on the side of the face. His temple bled as his knees buckled. I dropped the shovel and caught him so he wouldn't fall into view of the truck. Grady had binoculars, and I knew he would use them in a few minutes, if he wasn't already.

The gun slipped easily from Van's shoulder. The ammo pouch around his waist took a bit more effort to remove. Once I had both, I crept away, keeping the granddaddy tree between me and the workers until I could look back and not see a thing.

I didn't run, even though I wanted to. I crept along through the trees, not making any more noise than I could help. And, I listened. To everything. My heart hammered non-stop. By now, Grady would have found Van. There would be no peace after what I'd done, and I didn't want to find out what Oscar would do to me because of it.

It took forever for me to spot a house through the distant fields and even more time for me to make my way there under the cover of the barren branches. The field would have been easier, but I couldn't risk any of the guards driving by with the truck and spotting me.

The sun was high behind the clouds by the time I stood on the front porch. I took a calming breath and eased the door open. Going into an abandoned house to search for supplies wasn't new to me, but that didn't make it any less terrifying. My gaze never settled on any one thing as I scanned the front room.

Disregarding the light that shown through the windows, I reached for the switch. Nothing. That meant I needed to look for supplies and get out. I needed to find a place with lights to hole up for the night.

Silently closing the front door again, I moved forward. In the kitchen, I picked up a long knife—a smarter weapon—and shouldered the rifle.

Quietly, I searched each cupboard. Everything was empty. A door to the side of the kitchen drew my eye. Tall and narrow, I knew it probably led to a pantry. Just like I knew the smeared, dirty handprint beside the knob belonged to an infected.

Open the door and deal with the problem or walk away and potentially have a follower that might draw more? One I could handle. Two? Probably not.

I approached the door slowly, trying to quell the shaking in my hands. A small shuffle of noise behind me was the only warning I had. I whirled around, my arm already swinging forward. The infected opened his mouth just in time to swallow my blade.

Breathing hard, I twisted the knife and pushed up. The infected dropped like a rock. I pulled the knife from its mouth and looked over my fingers. No scrapes. No marks.

Something moved inside the food pantry. I took a kitchen chair and wedged it under the handle so the infected couldn't get out. The doorknob rattled as it tried, but the chair held. Alert not to make any noise that the infected would hear above its own, I moved on to check the rest of the house. Unfortunately, it had already been cleaned out by raiders.

In the basement, cluttered with old furniture and other junk, I found a canvas messenger bag hidden in one of the many plastic storage totes. I'd just slipped the strap over my head and let it settle on my shoulder when I heard an engine.

Through the basement's high, narrow windows, I saw the

truck approach.

I wanted to swear. Instead, I wedged my way between a musty sofa, a stack of totes, and a sewing mannequin. The engine died, and I waited.

Floorboards groaned overhead. I could hear the murmur of muted masculine voices but couldn't make out what was being said. I listened as whoever was up there moved around the house, checking room after room. Finally, steps scuffed on the stairs.

Someone swore and an explosion of noise made my ears ring. The mannequin stand beside me rocked.

"What the fuck? Are you trying to bring every infected around?" Grady said.

"I thought it was an infected. Let's go," a voice I didn't recognize said.

"She's here. You saw the chair."

"I agree she was here, but she's long gone by now. You saw what she did to Van. She's not stupid. She's going to keep running. So would I. Now, if you're done dicking around, we need to get back to the field to get Van to his dad."

I listened to the men go back upstairs. The truck started and the sound of the engine slowly faded.

It took me a moment to wiggle out of my spot before I cautiously hurried out of the basement. I knew I didn't have a lot of time. The gunshot and the engine would draw more infected, and I did not want to stab another one in the mouth without gloves.

After checking the yard, I slipped out of the house and made for the trees. The beat of my heart never slowed. I hated being outside. Exposed. In danger. Would this be it for the rest of my life? Always moving and watching over my shoulder? I hoped not. Yet, I didn't see how my life could be anything more than what it was now.

The bunker had proven that places existed where a person could hole up. But, I'd never considered the bunker safe. Not only was it filled with assholes almost as dangerous as the infected, there was only one entrance to the place. I'd watched herds of infected back when they were still stupid. They were easy to escape if you were smart. But some of them weren't stupid anymore. And, if some of the more intelligent ones found the bunker, the gunmen wouldn't be able to shoot their way out. Any humans would be stuck down there until they died.

I planned to be more clever than Oscar, though. I'd find a place with an escape plan, a surplus of food, and no people. Maybe then I'd feel safe.

Distant pops caught my attention, and I glanced south toward the direction of the field. Why were the guards firing? Because some infected found them or because they were purposely drawing more infected in to drive me toward them? Not taking any chances, I started looking for the next house. I walked for over an hour before I spotted one. The gunshots had faded, but it didn't make me feel much better. I didn't like that I could hear them at all. That the gunmen were still firing confirmed my suspicion they were drawing infected in. Idiots.

After watching the house for a long while, I crept across the yard and looked through the windows. The inside appeared as tossed over as the first house. I could stand going hungry for another day as long as there was light, though.

I eased the door open and listened for any noises before I reached in and tried the switch. Light flared in the room. I quickly turned it off and slipped inside, closing the door behind me. Room by room, I checked the place over. I didn't find any infected but discovered the water ran clear. With another scan of the room, I quickly washed my hands and my face then waited. No noise. I didn't allow that to lull me into letting my guard down as I started looking for any forgotten supplies.

The cupboards were bare like the last place, but I found two clear bottles in the recycling. I washed both with the soap I found under the sink then filled them with water. With the bottles safely tucked into my bag, I started my search of the second story. The beds were still neatly made in every room. I picked one with a clear view of the yard and a private bathroom.

Just as the sky started to dim, I turned on every light in the house and used a chair from the kitchen to block myself in the bedroom. I used the bathroom with the door open and the rifle right on the sink, within easy reach. It felt weird to wash my hands twice in one day. Even with the abundance of washing, my skin didn't quite come clean, though. Grit had stained my cuticles and nails.

A distant howl interrupted my contemplation of my dirty nailbeds and made me shiver.

Moving back into the bedroom, I sat against the wall across from the door. My stomach gurgled, a pathetic plea for food. I gave it a few gulps of water then checked the rifle and the box of ammo.

With a slow exhale, I set the rifle across my knees and stared at the door.

It would be a long night.

Three

The rattle of the doorknob jolted me awake. With my pulse thundering in my ears, I stared at the door. Early morning sunlight lit the room. I'd managed to stay awake through the night but must have fallen asleep just before dawn.

I'd just started to convince myself the rattle had been part of a dream when the knob rattled again. A low moan in the hall echoed the movement.

I swore silently then carefully stood, my rifle trained on the door. The shuffle of the infected's footsteps moved further down the hall where it tried another door. Exhaling softly, I moved to the window.

From the window, the front of the house looked clear. However, the porch roof directly below my room blocked a good portion of the view. For all I knew, there could be a herd of infected standing right by the front door. I hoped not.

With my rifle shouldered, I gently eased the pane up and removed the screen. Scuffs of noise came from below, and I wanted to hit something in frustration. Those assholes with their gunfire had succeeded in drawing more infected to the area. What had they been thinking? Hadn't they realized they would eventually need to come out of their bunker and deal with the mess they made?

The infected didn't really have an attention span per say.

They remained in the area until another noise drew them away. Oscar's crew had been lucky to claim the territory they had because there hadn't been many infected in it to begin with. Yesterday's shit trick had changed that.

Meanwhile, I had to figure out how to get around the infected below without being seen or heard.

Sweat beaded my upper lip as I eased myself out the window one leg at a time. On the roof, I carefully inched forward, wary not to scrape my foot against the shingles. I stopped as soon as I could see what I faced.

Four infected shuffled around right in front of the house. Easing away from the edge, I made my way to the back side of the wraparound porch. There, I waited for fifteen minutes before I eased myself over the side while holding my knife in my mouth. With a loose-kneed drop, I landed noiselessly on my feet.

My heart thundered in my ears as I took the knife from my mouth and sprinted soft-footed to the tree line. I'd almost made it when something slightly to my right caught my attention. Another infected lingered within the tree line in the direction I ran. Motionless, it watched me.

I didn't stop. I couldn't. If I changed direction, it would call out and bring the ones from the house. I ran right toward it, knife gripped tightly in my hand. Like the other infected, it opened its mouth just before I reached it, giving me a perfect target. Unfortunately, I didn't angle my knife enough. While I struggled to twist the blade upward and end its attempt to bring me to the ground, it called out.

The sound echoed from behind me.

I heaved, killing the infected I fought, then pulled my knife and ran like hell.

The calls grew in volume and number, almost drowning out the crunch of my passage through the trees. Ahead, I spotted another house and prayed. If it was clear of infected, I might just make it through this without a bite.

I pumped my arms and legs as hard as they would go and made it to the front porch before the infected cleared the trees. There was no caution when I entered. I threw the door open and startled a pair of infected. Dropping the knife, I brought my rifle up, fired twice, then sprinted for the stairs.

Before I reached the top, the house filled with calls. I opened the first door I came to and closed myself in. Finally, luck was on my side. The door actually had a lock. I used it and backed away, breathing heavily.

It took a lot of effort to tear my gaze from the door and quickly scan the room. A kid's bedroom. Twin bed. Dresser. Stuffed animals. I forced myself to check under the bed and in the closet. Infected free. Next, I checked the window. The porch on this house didn't reach the room I'd chosen. It was a good twelve foot drop to the ground, which I might have been able to handle without breaking anything, if the yard wasn't already crawling with infected. More emerged from the trees as I watched, drawn by the sounds of my gunfire and the calls from the ones already surrounding the house.

I was trapped until something else distracted the infected and they wandered away. It couldn't be more than nine or ten in the morning. I had time.

Sliding down the wall, I got comfortable and waited. The calls outside eventually quieted. Only the occasional scuff of noise in the hallway indicated they hadn't left yet.

I rationed my water and watched the patch of light on the wall slowly move across the room. Hunger gnawed at me, and I wondered if I'd be able to check the kitchen before I left.

When the light touched the bed, I got to my feet and checked the yard. My mouth dropped open at the number of infected milling around. A few stood still and watched the house. One saw me in the window and let out a call. It set off a chain reaction until their noise echoed in the house.

They weren't leaving. There was nothing else out there to distract them.

I stood there, still making eye contact, while realization settled over me. There would be no slipping away before dark.

"Shit."

Quietly crossing the room, I tried the switch. No lights. I had until dusk if the infected didn't figure out how to get into the bedroom before then. I couldn't decide which was the worst way to go. Eaten by a herd of infected or torn apart by a hound. A hound might be quicker.

I rubbed my face and swayed on my feet. Adrenaline and hope had kept me going. Without either, I stared at the door, half debating if I should just open it. Why put off the inevitable? It wasn't like anyone would find me and–

I looked at the window. After what I'd done to Van, returning would be hell. But, it wasn't like I had a choice. It was either give myself over to the raiders or be eaten, and I wasn't ready to die yet.

With determined steps, I moved to the window and slid it open. Aiming at the infected who'd met my gaze, I shot it right between the eyes. I paused for the count of three before killing two more. That was the distress fire pattern Oscar's gunmen had been taught to use if they were ever separated.

I waited and repeated the pattern again a few minutes later. The reports drew more infected from the trees, and I began to doubt my plan. Even if scouts from Oscar's group heard and came, how would they ever make their way through all of the infected?

A distant volley of five reached my ears a few seconds after my last shot. A mix of relief and terror gripped me. Now, I just had to wait. The shots hadn't sounded as far away as I'd thought I'd run, but everything was skewed when on foot and zigzagging through trees.

I moved to close the window and caught a glimpse of something dark moving very fast within the trees. A hound? My pulse spiked, and I jerked my gaze to the sky.

Since the earthquakes that brought them, hellhounds only came out at night. They feared light in any form. How could a hound be out already? I scanned the trees but didn't see dark movement again. The infected in the yard continued their loud calls, oblivious or uncaring about what lurked in the shadows behind them.

Spinning from the window, I scanned the room. The gunmen would never reach me in time. I needed something. A plan. A hiding spot. Something. But, there wasn't anything.

I looked up at the cracked ceiling and briefly wondered if I could break my way through and maybe find a crawl space. To go where, though? I couldn't live up there forever.

The hush in infected calls drew me back to the window. Disbelief robbed me of thought. Decapitated infected bodies littered the yard. Where ten had stood, none now moved. As I stared, a head came rolling into view. An infected awkwardly ran toward the trees from the other side of the house as if it were running from something. They never ran away.

"What the hell?" I said, softly.

In the hall, the infected grew louder. My stomach churned

as I turned toward the door and lifted my rifle. I did not want to know what was out there killing infected.

Thumps and grunts filled the air before only the sound of my harsh breathing remained. My everything shook, and I struggled to keep the rifle steady.

Someone knocked on the door, and my stomach flooded with relief a moment before it clenched with fear.

The wooden panel started to swing open, and before I'd fully decided how I wanted to greet Van, my finger spasmed on the trigger. Everything slowed as the boom filled the room.

A grey hand gripped the edge of the door and pushed it wide. My mouth dropped open at the sight of the man standing there. Gore covered every bit of clothing he wore, but that wasn't the cause for my shock.

He stood on two legs and wore human clothes, but he wasn't human. Grey skin covered every exposed bit of his body. His yellow-green reptilian gaze locked with mine. He smiled, showing enormous, pointy canines.

I remembered the rifle I held and lifted the barrel level with his head. Before I could fire it a second time, he crossed the room in a blur and pulled it out of my hands.

I flinched back and closed my eyes.

I'm too young to die, I thought.

"How old are you?"

It took a moment to realize the man had spoken to me. I opened my eyes in surprise.

"Wh-what?"

"You said you're too young to die. How old are you? And how old will you be when you die?"

I hadn't realized I'd spoken that out loud.

"I don't know." My eyes flicked to the rifle he still gripped, and I swallowed hard. He looked down at the weapon then tossed it onto the mattress before focusing on me again.

"You don't know how old you are?" His eyes slid over me from head to foot. "You don't look like a child. You look eighteen."

That glance reminded me way too much of Van, and I quickly shook my head.

The thing's shoulders slumped a little, and he reached out to pat me awkwardly on my head.

"It's all right. I will still keep you safe. My name is Ghua. What's yours?"

"Goo-ah?"

"Yes. Ghua. What's your name?"

"Eden."

"We need to leave, Eden. The hellhounds will be out soon, and this house has no light. It wasn't a good place for you to hide. Come."

He waved me forward, but I didn't move. I couldn't.

He saw my hesitation.

"I can't carry you because of all the infected blood." He waved at his messy clothes then picked up the gun. "You'll need to walk. I'm sorry."

I glanced at the gun again and nodded jerkily.

One step in front of the other, I made my way toward the door. There, I stopped. The hall was littered with body parts. Well, mostly bodies and heads, but I did see a separated arm wedge between the wall and the railing.

"Oh. Right. Wait here, and I'll clear a path."

He moved past me and started pushing the bodies down the stairs with his feet. I listened to the thud-thud-thud of a head rolling down before I turned and fled down the other end of the hall. The doors were open. A few dead infected lay on floors in those rooms as well. I reached the end of the hall and slowly turned, noticing the thudding and squishing noises had stopped.

Ghua waited at the top of the steps. His gaze locked with mine as he held the gun, the strap now on his shoulder.

"Come, Eden. It's safe now. The infected are off the steps."

He motioned impatiently. When I didn't move, he continued speaking.

"We don't have much time. There's a house with lights not far from here. We can stay there tonight so I can keep you safe."

He wanted to take me somewhere else? Hell no. But, the only way out of the hall was down those stairs, so I nodded and slowly walked toward him.

He showed me his teeth again, and I quickly looked away to focus on the blood-slicked stairs.

I considered it a miracle that I made it to the bottom using my feet and not my ass. Just when I was thinking of sprinting for the door, Ghua spoke from behind me.

"Wait here. Let me check the yard again. A few infected ran away."

I watched him walk out the door, then I pivoted and ran for the back of the house. The door opened easily, and I stumbled down the steps in my hurry to get away. Ahead, the trees beckoned. I just needed to get to them.

Ghua rounded the corner of the house at a jog, cutting off my escape route. I skidded to a stop and stared at him with wide-eyes.

"You should have stayed inside, Eden. It's not safe out here." His gaze dipped from my eyes to my heaving chest.

"How old do you think you are?" he asked, tilting his head to study me.

"Twelve." The response slipped from my mouth without thought; and as soon as I heard it, I couldn't believe I'd said it. There was no way he'd believe I was twelve.

"Six more years until you're eighteen." He sighed and nodded slowly. "I am a patient man, though. It will not seem so long."

I wasn't sure how to react. First of all, I couldn't believe he actually thought I was twelve. But mostly, the rest of his comment terrified me.

"What happens when I turn eighteen?"

"You will no longer be off-limits. Come. It's a long walk to the next house. We want to get there before dark."

I barely registered all of what he said. My brain was stuck on the first part. Off limits for what? And, he really expected me to go with him after he said that?

I glanced to my right and my left, wondering if I'd make it very far in either direction.

"Are you afraid of me, Eden?" he asked softly. "I am not angry that you shot me. I will not remove your head. I promise. Come on."

He motioned again. Numbly, I started walking. I'd seen all the separated heads in the house, but until that moment, it hadn't clicked he'd done all of that with his hands. I glanced at his biceps, clearly visible under the long-sleeved shirt struggling to encase his arms.

I couldn't go wherever he had in mind because I knew, once there, I'd have no chance of fending him off when he figured out I'd lied about my age. And, I was terrified what exactly he would do when I was no longer off limits. Was he another form of infected? Was this what the smarter ones were evolving into? Was I just a live snack for later?

"I'm so fucked," I said to myself.

Ghua stopped walking and slowly turned to look at me. The shock in his lizard eyes made me want to run. Instead, I stumbled to a halt.

"Children are not supposed to say that word."

I nodded quickly. "You're right. I'm sorry. I won't say it again."

"Good. When we get home, I will tell Mya you already knew the word. You did not learn it from me."

"Mya?"

"Yes. She is a human female, like you. The first one we found."

This guy was collecting us? My stomach sank as the rest of his words sunk in. There were more of him?

I needed to run, and I needed to run now.

Four

An infected called out somewhere nearby. Ghua put his hand up as if to stop me from walking although I hadn't started again.

"Stay here, Eden." He took off at a run to the east.

Heart racing, I immediately hauled ass to the west. Tree by tree, I put distance between me and the grey-skinned man. It sucked that he still had the rifle, but I'd manage with the knife. Just so long as I got away.

An infected moved out from a tree only steps in front of me. I reversed, almost falling on my butt and losing the knife.

The infected let out a low groan and lunged for me. I lifted my arms up, already visualizing how I would block and try to go for the broken branch to my right. However, that never happened.

A roar filled the air a moment before something dark jumped over me. The blur crashed into the infected and sent the body spinning horizontally, spread eagle. Its head connected with a tree and burst open like a ripe watermelon.

Stunned, I stared at the mess. The force of impact from that throw further kindled the fear I felt for the man herding me.

My gaze shifted to Ghua, who crouched in front of me. He watched the infected for a moment before he turned to me.

"Are you all right, Eden?"

He wiped his hand on his pants and reached for my face. His touch was gentle as he gripped my chin and nudged my head left then right for his inspection.

"The stupid human didn't bite you, did it?"

If I said yes, he might lose interest in me. However, I was also aware of the very real possibility that he might rip my head off before I turned into an infected.

I quickly shook my head no.

"Good. Mya said that children like to wander. I didn't know you could move so fast. I won't leave you alone like that again. It's too dangerous. That stupid human could have bitten you. You don't want to be stupid, too, do you?"

"No."

"I don't want you to be stupid, either. Stay close, and that won't happen."

I swallowed hard, knowing a threat when I heard one. The next time he started forward, he didn't need to motion for me to follow. I wouldn't be stupid enough to try to run like that again. I wanted to keep my head.

It didn't take long to reach the house.

On the porch, Ghua hesitated at the door and looked at me.

"You will need to follow me. But, stay close. There may be more stupid humans inside."

"Infected, you mean."

He tilted his head and studied me for a moment.

"You're a very smart child."

I shrugged slightly. "My friends called them infected."

He made a non-committal noise and opened the door.

For a brief moment, I considered taking off while he looked around. However, that thought fled when he flicked on the switch right inside the door. A hellhound wouldn't hesitate to attack me in the dark. This guy, however, hadn't done anything but kill infected. Hoping it stayed that way, I followed him over the threshold.

Other than electricity, I held little hope that the house had anything more to offer. The furniture in the living room was bloody, and every cupboard in the kitchen hung open. Not that Ghua let me stay in that area long enough to investigate further.

He herded me upstairs then used a twin mattress from the closest bedroom to block the hallway. While he wedged it into place, I checked the rest of the rooms. One had a possible escape route out the window and an adjoining bathroom. However, the water didn't run. I wasn't surprised. It'd gotten cold since that first attack. A few nights, it'd even dipped well below freezing. While scavenging, we'd found a few poorly insulated homes that hadn't yet had their heat on, which led to burst water lines.

I lifted the toilet tank's lid and refilled my water bottles from there.

"I didn't know that held water," Ghua said. "You are really smart."

My stomach clenched with fear and hunger. Was he catching on that I wasn't twelve? Was he just toying with me?

"I don't have a choice," I said. "If I'm not smart, I die."

He nodded and watched me guzzle down half a bottle of water. When I finished refilling it, I capped it and moved to drop it into my bag.

"Can I have some?"

I wanted to kick myself for not waiting until he slept to fill the bottles. I knew better than to openly display what supplies I had. That was the fastest way to get them stolen. Hopefully, he'd only take the one.

Sullenly, I held out the water bottle. He unscrewed the cap, chugged the contents, and handed me back the bottle.

We stared at each other for a moment while I waited for him to demand the other one.

"Thank you, Eden."

He turned and started looking in dresser drawers. We were in a girl's room. He took out a pair of jeans and held them up, studying them.

Not sure what to think of that, I refilled the bottle and put it in my bag before shutting the door to use the toilet. I made sure not to flush in case I needed what was left in the tank. When I reemerged, I found Ghua comfortably sitting against the door to the hallway. We were closed in the room together for the night.

Fear was a real motivator in my life. Fear of the hellhounds had me running for shelter long before sunset. Fear of becoming infected had kept me alert and ready to defend myself. Fear of becoming Van's next plaything had taught me when to use attitude to keep him at bay and when to keep my mouth shut.

Ghua was something to fear too. He'd ripped off heads like it was nothing, showing an aggression that would make armed men wet themselves. He'd threatened me and wanted me to come with him. But why? Without the why, I didn't know how to respond. I didn't know how to stay safe.

Again, we watched each other for a minute before I moved to the bed and sat down.

"Where are you taking me?"

"Home."

"Why?"

"To keep you safe."

"Why?"

He bared all his teeth at me. If they weren't so scarily sharp,

I might have thought he was trying for a wide smile.

"Now you sound like Timmy."

"Who's Timmy?"

"A child."

Ghua wasn't really giving me much. But, I knew I needed to find out more about him if I wanted to understand how to get away from him. So, I risked annoying him and kept trying.

"Where did you come from?"

"Ernisi. It's our home under the ground. Mom says our home is on the surface now, in Tolerance, near Whiteman."

Finally, a more substantial answer. Too bad I had no idea where Tolerance or Whiteman were, and my brain didn't want to wrap around the idea of him coming from underground because that rang too close to my imaginings of hell. So, I went with the safest bit of information.

"Your mom is with you?"

"She's not mine. She belongs to Mya. But Mom says we can call her Mom because we don't remember our own. Dad lets us call him Dad because Mom says so."

Belongs to Mya? The human he already captured?

"Are Mya's mom and dad human, too?"

"Yes. Some humans live with us, but most chose to stay at Whiteman." He looked away for a moment and rubbed his very pointed ear. My mouth dropped open a little at the sight of it. How had I missed a very elven-looking ear poking through his hair?

I closed my mouth before he looked at me again and tried to focus on our conversation. Humans. They had several already. That didn't bode well for me.

"The people you take get to choose where to live?" I asked.

"Take? I do not take people. I rescue them."

He met my gaze steadily, no trace of sly manipulation or deceit in his reptilian eyes. Probably because I had no idea what his tells were.

"So, if I wanted to leave right now, you'd let me?" I asked, not bothering to mask my doubt.

"No." He nodded toward the window. "It's getting dark. It's not safe to leave."

"And, in the morning? What about then?"

"It's not safe for a child to be alone."

Just as I'd thought. He wanted me to believe he was rescuing me, but he wouldn't let me go.

The first howl rang through the air outside, and I shivered at the sound.

"You are safe, Eden. Sleep."

"I'm not tired yet."

He stood and came toward me. It was then that I identified what was missing from the picture.

"Where's my rifle?"

"I used it to kill the first infected when you wandered away. It was too bloody to keep."

He reached around me and pulled back the covers.

"Lay down."

Even without the gun, he scared the hell out of me. Not wanting to appear openly defiant, I made a show of stacking the pillows and curling up on my side. I stared at him. He covered me with the blankets and went back to his spot at the door.

No way in hell was I closing my eyes.

* * * *

Even in my sleep, I understood the wrongness of feeling safe and warm. Warmth was a commodity that came at a high price, and safety was an illusion people felt just before they died. I struggled against the feelings and screamed at myself to wake up.

When my eyes finally opened, my heart was pounding hard. Weak daylight already lit the room. I recalled the hours spent listening to the distant hellhounds howl, but I couldn't remember falling asleep. I couldn't have slept for long. A few hours, maybe. But, even a minute had been stupid. What had Ghua done once my eyes were closed? What else might have found me?

I knew better than to fly out of bed to find out. Instead, my gaze scanned the room for infected first, then the grey man. Neither waited, but the door stood wide open.

Quietly, I sat up and swung my legs over the bed. My booted foot hit something with a thunk. I looked down at the can of dog food on the floor, and the rapid thump of my heart stopped for a beat. I recalled the very first time I'd turned around and saw a can of food on the street behind me. My parents had still been alive then. We'd been with the first group of raiders who'd "took us in." I hadn't realized it then, but I'd been lucky and escaped death that day.

My gaze drifted to the door, but there was no trail of cans leading out. Had there been, I would have known I was screwed.

A trail of food was one of the oldest infected tricks to lure a human into a trap. I hadn't known that, though, the first time I saw one. The infected hadn't shown signs of intelligence then; not like they did now. I'd collected all of the cans, following the trail from street to lawn to house without incident. I'd even raided a pyramid of perfectly stacked cans from the living room.

As I stared at the can on the floor, I recalled the one detail that had scared the crap out of me. That detail had taught me to avoid can trails in the future. When we'd left, I'd looked back and had caught a blur of something dark running away from the house. At the time, I'd thought it was a fast moving infected. Now, I realized what that blur had been. It was the same blur I'd seen in the trees just before Ghua had arrived to kill all the infected. I'd seen a grey man back then. Why had he left a can trail, though? It didn't make sense.

I picked up the can and tucked it into my bag. With my knife in hand, I cautiously crept to the door. The hall remained clear of infected, and the mattress still blocked off the stairs. Frowning, I checked the rest of the rooms. No Ghua and no infected.

I looked at the mattress. Smudges of dirt and old blood marred the surface where Ghua had grabbed it last night to shove it into place. What waited on the other side, now?

Shaking my head, I went back into the bedroom and looked out the window at the porch roof. It appeared to be the safer exit route. Like the day before, I popped the screen and climbed out to get a better feel for the state of things. No infected wandered the yard. I waited and listened for a scuff of noise beneath me. Heavy, grey clouds drifted in the sky; and a brisk wind made my time on the roof uncomfortable. However, no sounds came from below.

I dropped to the ground and looked around just as the first freezing rain drops fell. In this world, in order to survive, a few basic things were needed. A weapon. Something to carry water. Clothing enough not to freeze. And something to open a can of food. With only two of the four required necessities, I cautiously headed back inside.

The house didn't quite look the same as the night before. Headless bodies littered the floor. That was twice that the infected came into a quiet house at night. Either they could smell me, or they were now drawn by the lights and not just sound. Either way, the change didn't bode well for me.

I rummaged through the coat closet for something that would keep the rain off me and found a windbreaker large enough to go over my jacket. I put it in my bag as I headed toward the kitchen in search of a can opener. I moved quickly, the need to get away riding me hard.

The patter of the rain increased until it became a hushed roar of background noise. I hated rain. Not only could I freeze in it, but I wouldn't be able to hear a damn thing. While I searched, I kept vigilant, watching the doors and openings for infected, my knife always ready.

Just as my left hand closed around the can opener, a car door slammed outside. I panicked and looked around for somewhere to hide. Nothing stood out. I ran for the back door just as the front one opened.

"Eden," a familiar voice yelled.

I'd almost reached the back door when it, too, opened.

Ty, one of the gunmen from the bunker, lifted his rifle and leveled the barrel with my head. I came to a skidding stop.

"Eden," Steve, another gunman, said from behind me. "Don't try anything stupid. Drop the knife."

"Why are you here?"

Ty smirked but didn't lower his weapon. Something slammed into my hand. I cried out and involuntarily dropped my knife. Arms wrapped around me. Lifted off my feet, I kicked out with my legs and threw my head back in an effort to connect with something.

"You know why," Steve panted in my ear. "Settle down."

I kicked harder. There was no way I could go back with them. True, when I'd thought I might die, the bunker and its twisted occupants had seemed like a better option. But, things had changed. I was so close to setting out on my own again. With supplies.

The back of my head connected with Steve's face. He grunted and called for Ty. Ty turned his weapon, strode forward, and hit me in the head, just above my temple.

Dazed, my struggles went from make-you-bleed to entertain-you.

"Tie her hands and feet. It'll be easier to carry her out."

"No. Stop." I tried to move my hands out of reach but had a hard time thinking past the nausea and the pain in my forehead.

In no time, they had me bound and over Steve's shoulder. They walked toward the front door.

"What the hell happened in here?" Ty asked. "It looks like something ripped those infected heads right off."

"Probably the hellhounds," Steve said. "Hurry up."

They walked out into the rain. The chill helped clear my head a little.

"Why bother taking me back?" I slurred. "You said we wouldn't be going back to the fields. You don't need me."

"You need to start thinking long term, Eden. The infected and hellhounds aren't going away. We need to dig in and plan for the survival of humanity. There's a lot of work we'll need to do. We'll need all the workers we can get."

He carefully shoved me into the back seat. Laying on my side, I struggled to catch my breath and think. Ty closed the door, and they both got in front.

"You don't understand," I said, trying again. "Van's not going to forgive what I did to him. There's no point taking me back just for him to kill me."

"Oh, sugar, he won't kill you. He's mad, but you're too important to him," Ty said.

The engine roared to life, and the car started forward.

"What do you mean?" I asked.

"Like Steve said, we need to plan for the survival of humanity. You'll see that eventually and come around." Ty turned in his seat and looked back at me. "If you have your heart set on someone else, all you'll need to do is let Oscar know. Van doesn't have to be your only option."

"You're taking me back for breeding?" My stomach twisted, and I gagged. There was nothing to come up though. It had been days since my last meal.

Ty shook his head like I was being difficult and faced forward once more.

I studied the rope on my hands, then lifted them to my mouth to see if I could pick the knot out. They'd tied it off on the underside of my hands, though, making it difficult to catch an end of the rope with my teeth.

The car started to slow.

"What the hell is that?"

I leveraged myself into a sitting position to see what Steve was squinting at.

"Looks like a tree," Ty answered. "Go around it."

I looked out the rain-blurred window at the ditch beside the road. While there was no danger of the car tipping over, the ditch was deep enough that we wouldn't have an easy time getting out of it. Steve echoed my thoughts.

"We'll get stuck." He swore under his breath and hit the steering wheel. "I told Oscar we needed the truck."

"Calm down. It's a small tree. You cover me, and I'll move it."

The car rolled to a stop. Neither of them got out. We all watched out the windows. With the downpour, visibility wasn't great.

"Looks clear," Ty said.

We all knew it wasn't, though. Debris in the road was a standard infected tactic to stop a vehicle and get the passengers out where the infected could eat them.

"Let's go."

Steve opened his door first and got out. Rain blew in around him as he stood in the open door and looked around, his rifle ready.

"Hurry up. I can't see shit," he said.

Ty got out and closed his door against the wind and the rain.

With dread pooling in my stomach, I watched through the rain-distorted windshield as Ty jogged to the tree and tried to pull it from the road.

I shivered and, dismissing the rope that bound my hands, hurriedly lifted my feet to pick at the knot there. I needed to free my feet quickly because, without a doubt, this wasn't going to end well.

Five

Ty had barely moved the trunk of the tree two feet when the first infected sprinted from its hiding place. Steve brought it down with one shot, but the loud bang that filled the air made me wince. Even with the sound of the pouring rain, every infected within a mile would have heard the report.

Ty heaved at the trunk again. Something moved in the trees behind him. The dead infected hadn't acted alone.

A herd burst into view, and Steve swore. Even the best shot in the world couldn't provide enough cover to allow Ty to drag the tree the rest of the way off the road. Ty seemed to realize that, too, because he stopped his efforts and ran for the car.

Both he and Steve ducked back inside and slammed their doors shut seconds before infected reached us.

"Back up," Ty yelled.

Steve shifted into reverse and twisted in his seat to see out the back window. Not that it did him any good. The infected had already covered the car, rocking it back and forth as they beat against the sides and tried to push their way in.

Steve gunned it anyway. The vehicle bounced as he ran over a few infected, then the back end dipped down.

"Shit!" He slammed the shifter into drive.

"You ran into the fucking ditch."

"Shut up." Tires made noise under my seat, but we didn't

move.

While Steve and Ty yelled at each other, I watched the infected that stared in at us. Pale, milky eyes shifted from the two in front to me. I knew I was looking death in the eye again and again. There'd be no getting out of this mess.

"Don't shoot through the window. It's the only thing keeping them out."

I glanced at Ty, who was pointing his handgun at an infected staring at him through the windshield. The car rocked forward in Steve's attempt to get out of the ditch. Over the rev of the engine, we heard infected beating on the windows and roof.

A clunking noise came from my right, like someone's hand had slipped off the handle during an attempt to open the door.

"Lock the damn doors," I said, adding to the noise. "And untie me."

The locks slammed down while the car continued to rock. I could no longer tell if the motion was due to Steve's effort or the infected's.

The volume of groans outside the car increased, and blood exploded on the windshield. For a moment, I thought Ty had lost control and fired, but there was no hole in the glass.

We all looked straight ahead at the blood smeared spot in the press of decaying faces. One of the heads rolled out of sight, completely severed.

"Get us out of here," Ty yelled.

Chaos broke loose outside the car. Infected seemed to explode randomly, painting the glass with gobs of gore. Between that and the continued downpour, I couldn't see what else was happening. But, whatever it was, it wasn't good.

"What the fuck is out there? Is it a hellhound?" Steve fumbled for the windshield wipers. The smear of blood and water only further obscured the view of dark shapes churning near the hood.

A familiar roar filled the air, and my mouth dropped open in disbelief.

"Untie me." I shoved my hands right under Ty's nose. He shoved me back, and I tried for Steve next.

"Untie me," I demanded.

The low moans and grunts from outside stopped. The soft, rapid swish of the wipers filled the inside of the car along with Steve's panicked breaths. We all stared straight ahead as a familiar, huge form slowly rose.

"Shoot him," I said. "Shoot him."

Ty lifted the gun and fired. The bang echoed in the car, making my ears ring. But, I didn't flinch away from the noise. I couldn't. Frozen in my spot, I blinked at the empty spot where the grey man had stood.

"Where did it—"

The glass beside Ty's head burst inward, and he was ripped from his seat. The sound of his scream cut out, just like his words, as he disappeared through the gaping hole into the pouring rain. The gun he'd held fell to the seat.

The engine idled, any attempt to get us out of the ditch forgotten, as Steve and I both stared at the broken rain-filled window. My pulse thundered in my ears because I knew who was out there, but I still didn't know what he wanted.

Glass shattered again and jolted me into action like a starting whistle. I lurched forward, scrambling for the gun while Ghua slammed Steve's head into the steering wheel.

When the door to my left opened, I twisted and fired without taking time to aim. It didn't matter. There was nothing there to hit, anyway.

From outside came Ghua's disembodied voice, and he sounded angry.

"Eden, no. Shooting hurts."

Between one blink and the next, the gun disappeared from my grasp. Panting, I inched backward. With my hands and feet tied, I knew that escape wasn't going to happen. Yet, I couldn't just sit there.

As I stared at the open door and the lashing rain, his face appeared. Ghua. Water ran down his face, washing away the blood and bits from his beheading spree. The rivulets from the small temple braids weren't enough to clean his gore covered shirt, though. I shuddered at the gruesome sight of his brutal power.

His yellow-green eyes, with the vertical reptilian slit narrowed, locked on me.

"And, no more telling others to shoot me. Do you understand?" he asked.

I nodded.

He held out a hand and beckoned me forward. I almost shook my head in response; but after a quick glance at Steve, who was slumped forward against the steering wheel, I thought better of pissing Ghua off. I did not want to end up like Steve. Knocked out, I couldn't try to run.

I awkwardly scooted forward. Ghua's gaze shifted to the rope twined around my wrists, and he scowled.

"Why did they tie you?"

"Because I didn't want to go with them."

He grunted and squatted down so he could pick the knot free. I studied him as he worked. His gentle, warm touch felt wrong, given the headless bodies lying on the ground just behind him. Why did he keep coming back? I'd thought he'd left.

Once he had my hands free, I quickly untied my ankles while considering my options. Go willingly and maybe get another chance to run, or balk and get conked over the head. Or, worse, have my head removed. Not much in the way of options.

When I looked up, Ghua had his hand out again. My stomach quivered as I placed my hand in his. He didn't jerk me from the car as I expected but helped me out carefully.

The temperature and the rain leeched all the warmth from my hands and face within seconds. Teeth chattering, I reached into the bag still slung over my shoulder and withdrew the wind breaker. Holding it over my head, I looked up at Ghua.

"You are too cold. You cannot walk."

He looked down at his shirt, and I glanced at the car, wondering if he meant to drive it. Steve moved in the front seat, and my eyes widened.

"Come, Eden."

When I looked back at Ghua, he'd removed his gory shirt and had his upper body completely bare.

I started shivering harder just at the sight of him.

"Why aren't you wearing your shirt?"

"Infected blood is dangerous to you. It's safer to carry you like this."

"Carry me? Why? Where are you taking me?" I asked. "Back to the house?"

My string of questions made me want to cringe, but he didn't seem upset by them like Steve and Ty would have been.

"No," Ghua answered. "That house is not safe."

Before I could ask something else, he scooped me up into his arms and took off at a jog. I ducked my head against his bare chest and used the wind breaker as best I could to stay warm. It didn't help much. While the water-shedding material did keep my head and face dry, rain soaked my jeans and numbed my skin within minutes. I shivered hard in his arms and wondered if I'd die of hypothermia instead of something far more gruesome, like I'd figured.

The rain eased after another few minutes then tapered off to nothing. I stayed tucked in the windbreaker, my cheek pressed against his shoulder, the only source of warmth. Lifting my freezing hands, I set them against his chest. He grunted but kept running.

Exhaustion pulled at me, and I fought to keep my eyes open. I hadn't slept enough in the last few days. Between that and my dropping body temperature, I knew I was in trouble.

"I need dry clothes," I said, my lips struggling to form the words. "I'm too cold. I need to warm up or I might die. Please."

The wind grew stronger, chilling me further. I blinked slowly and turned my face further into Ghua's chest.

"I see a house, Eden. I will find you dry clothes."

His steps slowed, and I heard the echo of his tread on the porch a moment before he leaned over and set me down.

"Stay here, Eden. Do not wander. You need to warm up."

I managed to nod and listened to him break into the house. A head went flying out the door, followed by another. I closed my eyes, not wanting to see him clear out the infected. However, my eyes refused to open again when I tried, and I felt myself drawn toward the compelling need to sleep. To let go.

"Come, Eden." The rough, deep voice paused my descent into darkness.

Arms wrapped around me before I was gently lifted and cradled against a warm chest. I listened to the door close and his footsteps as he moved around in the house.

Ghua set me down on something soft, and his hands

immediately went to the zipper of my jacket. As he worked it down, I struggled to remember why I should tell him to stop. Sure, he had grey skin and eyes that freaked me the hell out. And, he also liked to rip off heads and had very sharp teeth. He probably wasn't the most likely source of help. But, in that moment, I couldn't recall why anything mattered more than how cold and tired I was. Did it really hurt to accept help every once in a while?

His hands pushed the jacket wide and gently worked my arms from the sleeves. Then, he stopped touching me.

"You do not look like the children at Whiteman."

Those words gave me the reason I should have undressed myself and started my heart beating harder. Ghua thought I was a child, and that belief was keeping me "off limits" in his mind. From what? I didn't know, and I didn't want to find out. However, I might not have a choice now. He'd removed my jacket and could see that I had breasts because of the way I was laying on my back.

I strove to open my eyes and won the battle after a moment. He was staring down at my chest, a confused look on his face.

"T-twelve is-s between ch-child and adult," I managed to say.

He grunted and turned away from me to start looking through drawers. I exhaled in relief when he found some pajama pants and a sweatshirt that looked like they would fit me.

I tried to sit up but couldn't manage on my own because of the shivering. Ghua noticed my struggles and put an arm under my shoulders to help me up.

"I c-can t-take it from here," I said.

He nodded, set the clothes next to me, and with one last

look, left the room. I kicked off my boots, wondering what I would find when I peeled off my socks. The toes weren't black like I'd suspected, just really pale. After a moment rubbing them, I stood and fought my way out of my wet jeans. By the time they landed on the floor, I collapsed on the bed, ready to sleep. The shivering had slowed but not because I was warm.

"Are you done changing, Eden?"

Ghua's voice sounded much too close.

"I need just a second."

Not daring to remove my wet underwear, I worked the pajama pants on an inch at a time. The damp shirt came off next, quickly replaced by the dry sweatshirt.

"I'm done." I wasn't sure if I said it to him or myself because I had no strength left to put on anything else. I lay back down and closed my eyes.

"We cannot stay here, Eden," Ghua said as soon as he walked in. "There is no second floor and no electricity." I listened to another drawer open. His warm hands picked up my feet. "You are still too cold."

"I know."

He grunted and continued to hold my feet, slowly warming them. Once they no longer felt like blocks of ice, he put two layers of fluffy socks on. Then, he flipped the edges of all the bedding over me and wrapped me up like a taco. I didn't protest when he picked me up like that and walked out of the house.

The rain hadn't started again, but the dark skies didn't bode well for me staying dry for long. Ghua immediately started running again. I burrowed my head under the blankets and, against my better judgement, closed my eyes.

He didn't let me sleep, though. Over the next hour, he tortured me in various ways. Sometimes he would start talking to me and wouldn't stop until I answered. Other times, he would uncover my face and jostle me while whispering my name. The only way to make him stop was to open my eyes and glare at him. His response to that was to touch his forehead to mine briefly and then bury my face in blankets again.

My blanket cocoon hadn't really warmed me any. I still shivered when I was awake, but that eased up each time I started drifting off. I knew what that meant, just as I knew why, during that hour, he also set me down for a few minutes only to pick me up and start running again.

Finding a warm, safe place to crash for the night no longer mattered to me. Just like getting warm no longer did, either. I was giving up. And, that was okay.

My teeth stopped chattering a few moments after he set me down for the umpteenth time. I was on the cusp of giving into sleep when Ghua grabbed me up again and shook me a bit harder than necessary.

"We will stay here." Shake. "Do you hear me, Eden? I found a safe house with water and electricity." Shake. "Open your angry eyes. Now." Shake.

I gave in and opened my eyes to glare at him.

"Go away."

"No." He leaned in and set his forehead to mine. The warmth of his gusty exhale bathed my face.

"Do not close your eyes again. You are too young to die. Remember?"

Six

Remember? How could I not? However, all the world offered lately was death or misery. Why should I keep fighting so hard to live?

"No, Eden," Ghua said, jostling me again.

I felt him moving, but I had closed my eyes again and couldn't see where he was taking me. Not that I cared.

He sat, settling me in his lap, before he unwrapped the blankets from around me and began to briskly rub my arms.

"Leave m-me alone." I mumbled the words and weakly lifted my hand to bat him away.

He caught my hand and rubbed some heat into my fingers. How could his hands be so warm? I stopped fighting his hold and sighed, relaxing against his chest.

"Humans do not heat as well as we do," he said as he focused on the other hand. "You need thicker clothing and more blankets. Drav told me that Mya sometimes still gets cold even with both."

He released my hand and set his palm against my cold cheek. Everywhere he touched warmed, but as soon as he lifted his hand, my skin immediately cooled.

"You are not heating yourself at all." His hand left my cheek and slipped under my sweatshirt to lay against my belly. He grunted when he touched my cold skin. I should have tried batting him away again, but his warmth felt too good.

"Children and the old ones are more fragile. I should have been more careful with you."

He leaned me forward, gripped the bottom of my sweatshirt, and tugged it up and over my head before I could squawk in protest. The bulky steel bands he called arms wrapped around me and pulled me against him once more. The heat of his chest branded my back. I started to shiver again.

"W-what are you doing?"

"This is how Drav warms Mya. Well, he does other things, but I cannot do those things with you until you're eighteen."

I almost couldn't think after that statement. He sure made it sound like they weren't interested in humans as a food source. The alternative almost scared me more.

"Are you saying they have s-sex?"

"Yes, but children are not supposed to talk about that."

He tucked my head under his chin and held me close. Other than the skin to skin contact of his chest to my back, he kept to himself as he continued to smooth his hands down my arms. After what he'd just revealed and his comments about "off limits" until eighteen, I knew he truly believed I was a kid. But how?

"Are human children that different from yours? Are yours hatched fully grown or something?"

He chuckled.

"No. We do not hatch children. We have no children. None that we can remember. No females or elderly, either."

"So there's just a bunch of guys like you?"

"Yes."

That made my stomach clench with worry.

"How many?"

"Mya thinks about two hundred."

Whoever this Mya was, she seemed to talk to these guys a lot. Not that I blamed her. If given the choice between talking and having sex with one of them, I'd talk his damn ears off about anything and everything.

"Turn so I can warm your feet," he said.

I moved on his lap and sighed at the contact of his chest and my side. He reached down and peeled the two layers of socks off my feet. The feel of his warm fingers on my cold toes would have been enough to make me moan, but then he started massaging them. I couldn't stop the noise that came out of me as I snuggled closer.

His fingers stilled momentarily, then he resumed without comment.

As I warmed, my head began to hurt. I gingerly touched the spot where the butt of the gun had connected and felt a small egg. Asshole Ty. My anger at being hit shifted to worry as I recalled the way Ty had disappeared out the window. Not worry for Ty but for myself.

"Can I ask you some questions?" I asked Ghua.

"You wouldn't be a child if you didn't."

I could hear the humor in his voice, but the statement still worried me. What would happen if he found out I'd lied?

"Why did you come for me after Steve and Ty took me?"

"I thought you'd wandered off and was looking for you when I heard the gunfire."

If only those two wouldn't have found me, I might have managed to get away. Instead, their stupidity had likely gotten them killed. Another thought interrupted that line of thinking. Ghua hadn't left me. At least not with the intent of never returning. Given his comment about sex, which I didn't want to think about, it made sense that he'd been looking for me. His reaction, when he found me, puzzled me though. Had he been protecting me?

"Why did you attack the guys who took me?"

"They shot at me."

I couldn't help but feel a small stab of disappointment.

"So did I." I wanted to kick myself for reminding him of that fact when his hand stilled on my foot.

"You didn't know any better, but you do now, right?"

I nodded quickly, and he resumed warming me while I internally freaked out more. His response had answered any question I had about what would happen when he found out I lied.

"Can I get up?"

"You're still cold." His hand continued to knead my foot.

"I know. But I'm hungry too."

He released my toes, stood, and set me on my feet in one fluid move. He didn't step back as he looked down at me. Eyes wide, I crossed my arms over my bra and met his gaze.

"I can only keep you safe if you stay close to me. Do you understand?"

I nodded, and he bent to pick up my sweatshirt. I didn't miss the way his gaze darted to my crossed arms before he handed the shirt to me.

"Come. We'll search the kitchen for food. Make sure you do not go near the windows."

He turned away, giving me a moment to yank the sweatshirt over my head.

"Ready," I said when I was covered.

He glanced back at me then led the way out of the cozy, clean living room to the kitchen. This house appeared untouched by scavengers. I itched to search through the cabinets for myself, but my shaky legs demanded I sit at the center island instead.

Ghua opened cupboard after cupboard. He found dishes, counter appliances, spices, but no food.

“Try that long cabinet by the fridge. It’ll either hold the broom, mop, and garbage or—”

I grinned at the sight of cans and cans of food.

“Which one should I open?” he asked, glancing at me.

“Pick one of the ones with the red and white label.” I was so hungry I wasn’t hungry, if that made sense, and I was afraid anything heavier than soup would make me sick.

Ghua pulled the tab on top of the can and poured the chicken noodle soup into a pot on the stove. Without me having to tell him, he added a can of water and correctly turned on the burner.

“You know how to cook?”

“Yes. Mom and Mya are teaching us.”

“Why?”

“So when we leave to search for survivors, we know how to feed the ones we find.”

I considered him for a moment. The way Ghua had worded it, he made it sound like he was willing to “rescue” any guy or girl he found. Yet, his interest in my age and glances at my chest had me wondering if he was just another version of Oscar’s men. A scarier version.

“If you’re wandering around looking for people to save, why didn’t you take Steve and Ty, too?”

“They were too afraid. They would have kept trying to shoot me.”

“Like me?”

He grunted and stirred the soup. In my mind, his response

confirmed my suspicion. He was after women. He already talked about Mya and her mom a lot. Deciding not to push, I changed the subject.

"Did you kill Ty?"

"No. Mya doesn't like it when we kill humans. She says they only shoot at us because we scare them. They don't mean to challenge us."

"Challenge?"

"Yes. A challenge is a fight to prove our strength. Now that we are on the surface, we can no longer remove heads during a challenge. Mya and Molev agreed we should arm wrestle while we are here. It's not as enjoyable, but it is entertaining to watch the humans try to move our hands to the table."

"Um, okay." He made it sound like he'd been around a lot of humans. How many had he already found? I recalled him mentioning a place where the humans he rescued stayed. He'd called it Whiteman.

"What's Whiteman like?"

"It is like a city but with tents instead of houses. The humans live in them. The base has some electricity. Enough for the lights that keep the hellhounds away."

"Base? You mean a military base?"

"Yes."

He turned off the soup and poured it into two bowls while I tried to figure out what it meant that these grey guys were interacting with people at a military base. Maybe there was more out there than raiders fighting over supplies. Maybe these grey guys actually were on our side and really were helping people like Ghua said. Or maybe not. Maybe he meant they'd taken over the base and now used it as some kind of harem camp for the female survivors they were collecting.

Given everything Ghua had told me so far, the latter seemed more likely.

"How long will it take to get to Whiteman?"

"I'm not sure. If I ran with you straight through, maybe a day. But you get too cold when I run, so, two, maybe three, days."

"What will happen to me when I get there?"

He set my bowl before me and tilted his head as he studied me.

"Happen?" he asked.

"Yeah. Am I going to be put to work? Auctioned off to whichever male has the most money."

The vertical slits in his eyes narrowed sharply, making my heart thump harder.

"You will not work, and you will not be auctioned. I found you. I will take care of you."

"And when I turn eighteen?"

He turned away from me to grab a spoon from the drawer.

"It is not a subject for children."

Well, that pretty much answered my question. My stomach churned. When I turned eighteen, I would no longer be off-limits to Ghua. How had I managed to escape one sex-on-the-mind guy just to be found by another?

I took my first spoonful of soup and tried to ignore the panic attempting to consume me. Swallow by swallow, I ate and considered my options. I'd almost gotten away once. I needed to try to run again.

While I finished what remained in my bowl, Ghua searched the drawers until he found a washcloth. Keeping in mind his warning to stay close, I stood and brought my dishes to the sink while he wet the cloth. Before I turned to go back to my seat, he caught my chin in his hand and gave my face a quick swipe.

Stunned, I could only stare as he shifted his attention to washing my fingers.

"You're clean." He set the cloth aside and scooped me up in his arms.

"How many kids are at Whiteman?" I asked as he carried me back to the living room and sat in the overstuffed chair.

He tucked the blankets around us before settling back. Pinned against his chest, this time with my sweatshirt on, I waited for his answer.

"Not many. There are a few boys your age. Some girls a little older—but they don't look like you—and some very small children, who fall down a lot."

"Only the ones who fall a lot need their faces washed for them. The rest usually manage on their own."

"I know."

"Then why did you wash my face?"

"Because I like taking care of you."

That's what I'd been afraid of. Not knowing what to say or do, I held still on his lap while he rubbed my arm through the blanket.

The heat of his bare chest and the soup in my belly gradually warmed me. It was unsettling, cuddling in his lap like that, but if I were honest with myself, I hadn't been so comfortable in a very long time. The slow sweep of his hand lulled me, and my eyelids began to droop. I gave in and closed my eyes, knowing that I was safe enough…for now.

I didn't sleep too long. I never did. Even back in the bunker, sleep left a person too vulnerable. So, when I opened my eyes again, the light in the room had only faded a bit.

Ghua reclined beneath me, his hand no longer petting my

arm through the blankets. The steady beat of his heart under my head had slowed, as had his breathing. I moved a little and waited to see if he'd wake up. His heartbeat and breathing remained steady.

Careful not to wake him, I eased out of the blankets and off his lap.

This was my chance to run again. But I couldn't run out of the house like I was. I'd lost all my supplies when he'd stripped me in order to get me into dry clothes. Even my boots.

Tiptoeing, I went to the front closet by the door. Luck was finally on my side. Not only did the door open noiselessly, I also saw winter coats and boots close to my size. I did an internal happy dance and pulled out what I would need. On the top shelf, I also found a backpack. This house was the jackpot for supplies. I'd walk out fully clothed so I wouldn't freeze, and I'd also be able to cram the backpack full of food and grab a knife from the kitchen.

With a grin on my lips, I slipped on the jacket and placed the boots in the pack. It would be safer to put them on once I was outside. I didn't want to make noise walking around while I gathered the rest of what I needed.

I turned, ready to creep into the kitchen, and discovered my luck had only been an illusion.

Ghua studied me from his relaxed position on the chair. His gaze dipped to the backpack in my hands, and my stomach twisted. He'd caught me once and only scolded me. I prayed he'd take it easy on me again since he thought me a child.

He stood slowly and stalked toward me, his gaze never leaving mine. I could see it in his eyes. He knew what I'd been about to do.

He stopped before me and lightly ran his fingers along the

furred edge of the coat's hood, from forehead to jaw. The palms of his hands brushed my cheek, and I suppressed a shiver at the sensation, terrified of moving.

When he reached my neck, he spread his hands wide and brushed the coat off my shoulders. The sleeve of my left hand caught on my fist. His steady gaze held mine as he waited for me to decide what to do about the horded supplies gripped in my hand. I dropped the bag with a thud. He finished removing the jacket and placed it back in the closet, along with the bag and boots.

Facing me, he held out his hand.

"Are you hungry?"

I looked down at his offering. I wasn't stupid. He was giving me a chance to pretend that I hadn't been about to leave him. Again. But why? I glanced up at him, meeting his pale green gaze. I couldn't read anything in his expression. No anger. No amusement, either.

Swallowing hard, I managed a nod and slipped my hand in his.

"You'll learn to trust me," he said. "I know you're afraid. I can hear the way your heart beats so hard every time you look at me. To you, I look like a monster. To me, you are the most wonderful thing I've seen."

The heart he could apparently hear went into overtime at his admission.

He exhaled heavily and gripped the back of my neck with his free hand. Slowly, he leaned down until his forehead touched mine.

"I will protect you, Eden. Even from yourself."

After a moment, he released me and pointed to the kitchen. Without needing to be told twice, I scurried ahead of him and plopped down on the same stool as before.

Seven

Ghua appeared completely at ease as he walked to the pantry cabinet. I was wound so tightly I thought I'd explode.

What had he meant when he said he would protect me from myself? What was he going to do? He hadn't yelled or hurt me or even threatened me. I didn't know what that meant either.

"Which can should I choose?" he asked, looking back at me.

Nervous guilt made it impossible to meet his gaze. I swallowed hard, not even remotely hungry, and glanced away. My gaze landed on the refrigerator.

"Since the power's still running, we should probably check the freezer."

"Show me."

Was this his form of punishment? I would rather have him yell than make me open a fridge that hadn't been touched since the world went to shit. I'd had to do that too many times already. None of them had ended well.

Reluctantly, I got off the stool and went to the fridge. Holding my breath, I opened the main part first. As I'd guessed, there was a lot of spoiled food. However, most of the moldy items were safely trapped within containers, so I resumed breathing normally.

"What is that?" Ghua reached around me to go for one of the fuzzier objects.

I realized he truly had no idea what we were looking at and grabbed his arm to stop him.

"You don't want to open that. It'll smell awful. When the food's fuzzy, it's already gone bad."

He curled his hand in a fist, and I quickly released him and took a step back to close the door. My back bumped against his chest, and the arm I'd just released snaked around my waist to hold me steady.

"Your heart is racing again. There's no need to fear me. I will not hurt you, Eden."

I closed the door and turned to face him. He was too close. Angry and afraid, I retreated until my back touched the fridge.

"You won't hurt me, but you won't let me go, either. You want something from me but tell me I'm too young to understand what that is. The world has completely changed, and I understand a whole lot more than you think. I don't want to have sex with anyone, and knowing that you're waiting for me to be old enough, scares the hell out of me. Let me go."

For a long moment, he said nothing. My heart continued to thunder in my chest while he studied me.

"Where would you go?" he asked finally.

He had me there.

"I don't know. Someplace safe where people aren't trying to force me to do things I don't want to do. Somewhere I can just be left alone."

He looked at me sadly and gently reached up to touch my cheek.

"Alone is a terrible thing to feel. It brings an emptiness that eats you from the inside. It leaves you desperate and hollow. It makes you wish for death even when death will not come. I've lived many lives. Each one more alone than the last. You don't want that."

"I do."

He sighed and dropped his hand.

"I will not force you to do anything no matter what age you are. But, I will take you somewhere safe. A place where people won't force you to do things you do not want to do."

I didn't believe him. Not for a moment.

"Okay." I motioned him away. "Let me check the freezer."

He stepped back enough so I could turn around and pull out the lower freezer drawer. I found several packages of steaks, which made my mouth water, and a package of cheese-filled ravioli.

"Jackpot!" I pulled everything out and excitedly started looking for the pot and pan I'd need. I didn't even care that we couldn't grill the steaks. It had been ages since I'd had any real, red meat.

Ghua stayed out of my way as I moved around the kitchen, and it was easy to forget he was even there until it was time to plate everything up. I divided the food and slid a plate with three seasoned steaks and a heaping portion of ravioli his way.

Without waiting for him or bothering to sit, I dug in.

A moan escaped me at the first bite of medium rare meat. How had I thought I wasn't hungry? Chewing greedily, I swallowed in a rush so I could shove the next piece in my mouth. Bite after bite, I consumed the first steak then the second. Juice dribbled down my chin and I wiped it away with my sleeve, barely pausing. The ravioli tasted just as divine. By the time I'd cleared my plate, my belly ached.

I looked up and found Ghua watching me with concern.

"I did not know you were so hungry. I'm sorry, Eden. Do you want mine?" He started to push his untouched plate toward me.

The actual concern in his voice surprised me.

"No. I'm good now. Thank you."

He nodded then slowly began to eat his steak.

While he ate, I went to the pantry and started sorting through the canned goods. His assurance that he wouldn't force me to have sex with him hadn't changed a thing. I still planned to run because I knew people lied. It had happened a lot before the hellhounds. But, after the hellhounds, that was all people did. Lie to trick a family into forced labor. Lie to steal supplies from other people. Lie just to live, like I was doing. It was the way of the world.

Anything protein based went on the counter. Those cans would keep me full longer than any cans of vegetables would. The snack packs of apple sauce caught my eye, and I put those on the counter too.

"Do all children like applesauce?" Ghua asked.

"Yeah, I guess so."

He grunted in acknowledgement and continued to watch me make a stack of cans. He didn't stop me, and that gave me hope.

"Can I put these in the backpack? For tomorrow?"

He gave me a knowing look that made me want to squirm. He might be clueless about some things, but he knew damn well I was still thinking about running. He surprised me by nodding, though.

After fetching the bag from the closet, I loaded it with cans and tested its weight. I'd never be able to run with that much without making a ton of noise. Depressed, I started removing a few cans.

"Why are you taking them out again?"

"It'll be too heavy to carry with all of those cans."

"No. It won't. Fill it with whatever you want. I will carry your food so you do not go hungry again."

And so I wouldn't run away. He was good at this game, but I was better. I put the cans back in the bag, organized so the ones I didn't want would be near the top and easy to ditch when I got another chance to run.

"Come. We need to go upstairs. It's getting dark." He held out his hand to me.

To keep the peace and hopefully assuage his suspicion, I placed my hand in his. His fingers curled around mine, and he led me out of the kitchen, turning on each light we passed on our way upstairs. He did the same on the second floor until every room was lit up.

At the end of the hall, he left me with a firm, "stay here." While he went to stuff a twin mattress in the opening of the stairway, I checked the master bedroom's possible escape routes. The bedroom windows were big enough to fit through but too far from the ground to jump safely. I'd do it if it was a choice between life and death, but that wasn't what I was facing at the moment.

Turning, I studied the rest of the room. With a pang of regret, I took in the nice decorations and comfortable looking bed. The cozy world this room belonged to was gone. The best the bed would see now was my rank, fully clothed body lying on top of the covers. I wished it could be different, though. I wished I could go to bed clean and comfortable for a change. Just as I wished doing that wouldn't be the quickest way for me to die.

It wasn't just closing my eyes that made me vulnerable at night. In this new world, there was no sleeping under covers that could tangle you up and slow your escape. There sure as hell was no sleeping without boots and a jacket on. Yet, I'd be doing both tonight.

I sighed and walked to the connected bathroom. A quick search of the closet there didn't turn up any new packs of toothbrushes, not that I'd really expected to find any. Finding new toothbrushes was like finding gold. Most of those kinds of supplies were in towns big enough to have stores. And, a town was a place I'd never go.

Turning, I faced the holder on the pristine counter and plucked up one of the used toothbrushes. In the old world, I would have never dreamed of using someone else's toothbrush. In this new world, I was lucky to have soap nearby to clean it first. With paste on the bristles, I scrubbed my teeth thoroughly, just happy that I could finally brush them after three days of going without. I spit and stuck my hand into the water to rinse. The water was actually warm.

Turning off the tap, I glanced at the shower over the tub. It wasn't anything special. Not huge or with seven fancy showerheads, but it looked like heaven.

"You can shower if you want," Ghua said from the doorway, startling me. "We have time before the sun fully sets."

My gaze shifted between him and the shower. Could I? Should I? Everything itched. A lot. And, even after getting drenched, my smell could kill a pony. I wanted a shower beyond belief but not at the risk of being raped as soon as I had my clothes off. He had, after all, just told me I was the most wonderful thing he'd ever seen.

"I'd rather not," I lied.

He studied me for a moment, grabbed the doorknob, and started pulling the door closed with him on the outside.

"There's a lock on the door. You have fifteen minutes before the sun sets."

With that, he finished closing the door.

I frowned and chewed my lip for a moment. Was I honestly considering showering despite the big, grey risk on the other side of the door? Just living each day brought danger. Did I really want to die dirty? No. I didn't want to die at all. And, I wouldn't because I wasn't weak or timid. I was strong, and more importantly, I was smart. I made things happen. My way.

Opening the door, I found Ghua sitting against the bedroom's only exit. His gaze shifted from the window to me.

Pretending he wasn't there, I crossed the room and started searching through dresser drawers. The woman's clothing I found would be a bit loose, but it would work. With a clean change of clothing, I closed myself into the bathroom.

The first time I shampooed my hair, the soap didn't foam up because my head was that greasy. I washed and rinsed three times before I conditioned then soaped my body. It was paradise standing under what felt like an endless supply of hot water. I never wanted to leave. Because of that, I stayed too long.

The door opened. How could I have forgotten to lock it? I panicked and looked around for a weapon. None of the bottles were big enough to do any damage.

"Eden, you need to turn off the water, now. We don't want the hellhounds to hear us or they will keep you awake all night with their noise."

The door clicked shut again.

I scrambled to turn off the water so I could hear him coming. The only thing I heard was the drip-drip-drip from my hair in the sudden absence of noise. No whisper of movement reached my ears. Heart thudding, I gripped the curtain and peered around it to find myself alone in the steam-filled room. He'd left? Relief flooded me.

Quickly drying with the softest, cleanest towel I'd seen in weeks, I dressed before he changed his mind. When I opened the door, I once again found Ghua blocking the only exit.

"Do you want me to brush your hair?" he asked, his gaze sweeping over me.

"No. I got it."

I left the door open so I could keep an eye on him while I detangled my hair.

Once I finished, I left the bathroom and went to lay on the bed.

Ghua stood, and I immediately sat up.

"What are you doing?" I asked when he started coming toward me.

"Tucking you in. You need to be under the covers to stay warm."

He picked me up with one arm, pulled back the covers with the other, and set me on the clean sheets. I shook my head mutinously when he motioned for me to lay down.

"I don't want to be under the covers."

"Why do children never want to do what they are told?"

"Genetics."

He grunted and planted his palm on my forehead, forcing me to lay back. Before I could protest, the covers were drawn to my chin.

"Sleep, Eden."

As soon as he turned around, I rolled to my side so I could watch him return to his spot. He sat against the door and, like the night before, closed his eyes.

Against my better judgement, I remained snuggled under

the covers.

* * * *

I stretched my legs, cracking my ankles, before I curled back up and burrowed closer to the warmth behind me. I was so glad the alarm hadn't gone off yet. I wanted just five more minutes of sleep. Five more minutes of snuggling with—

My eyes popped open, and I stared up at the strange, yet familiar, room. I knew right where I was and who had his arm casually wrapped around my waist. My head wasn't even on a pillow but on the bulky bicep of his other arm.

Ghua was full-on spooning me. I elbowed him hard and quickly scrambled out from under the covers.

He sat up and watched me with confusion in his gaze.

"Do you have to go to the bathroom?" he asked quietly.

"Why were you in bed with me?"

"Comforting you."

"Bullshit."

"Eden, children don't say that word."

"Ghua, grown men don't spoon children."

"I was not spooning. I did not touch places I was not supposed to touch. I was snuggling so the hounds would not wake you. You moved less when I held you close."

I glanced at the window. The sun was well up.

"Why didn't you stop snuggling when the sun rose?"

A low infected call came from somewhere downstairs.

"I thought the infected would scare you too."

The doorknob to our room rattled, and Ghua sighed and got off the bed.

"Go into the bathroom and close the door. They must have figured out how to get around the mattress." He moved to leave.

"Wait!" There was no way I would lock myself in the bathroom of a house full of infected without having some kind of weapon with me.

I ran to the closet and started ripping clothes off their hangers. Ghua said nothing as I pulled out the bar that used to hold the clothes.

He nodded when I turned.

"Do not open the door until I tell you it's safe."

With the thick wooden rod in hand, I hurriedly closed myself in the bathroom.

The wait seemed endless as I listened to thumps and sounds of shattering glass that echoed around the house. From the first floor, the infected calls swelled then died completely.

I bit my lip and stared at the door. No knock came. What if he didn't come back? What if they killed him? At least he'd left the lights on to keep the hounds away. I'd have a chance. But, I'd still be trapped in the bathroom for days, waiting for the infected to lose interest.

Ghua's sudden knock made me jump.

"The infected are dead," he said through the panel, and relief flooded me at the sound of his voice.

"You can come out and sit on the bed," he continued. "Do not touch anything. They made a mess."

I opened the door, ready to thank him, but stopped short at the sight of him pulling his pants off. Blood covered his hands and face, but I barely paid any attention to those details. My focus stayed locked on what hung between his legs.

My hand twitched on the rod I still held. The pathetic piece of wood had nothing on the large, grey penis that now swung freely for all to see. And boy did I see it. How could I not?

Ghua's two hands attempted to cover his man parts. It

wasn't enough. The head still peaked just below his fingers. If he was this massive flaccid...

"Eden. Children should not look there."

I swallowed hard and looked up to meet Ghua's troubled gaze.

Eight

For several long seconds, we just stared at one another. Me with my rod tightly gripped in my hand and Ghua with his rod barely covered. Knowing that he wanted me to grow up so he could do things to me with that scattered my rational thought patterns.

"Eden, go sit on the bed. I need to wash away the infected blood." He motioned with his head that I should get out of the bathroom doorway. Meanwhile, his hands remained firmly cupped over his—I didn't even know what to call it. Penis seemed too underwhelming of a term.

"Eden," he said again.

I nodded numbly and moved toward the bed, passing him while trying to put a name to the grey nemesis he had failed to conceal. Womb Raider? Vlad the Impaler? Dongzilla?

"The door will stay open so I can hear you. No looking."

He turned and strode into the bathroom while I unabashedly stared at his hard ass. His muscles had muscles. How did I ever think I would get away from him?

The shower curtain rasped open and closed as I sat on the mattress. A second later, the water turned on and the sound removed the fog in my brain. What was I doing? He'd cleared the house and was in the shower where I knew it was hard to hear much of anything. I needed to move now.

I stood and raced downstairs. Bodies and heads lay everywhere. I didn't stop to think or look. I went straight for the closet, almost tripping in my hurry. The sound of the water running upstairs acted as a timer as I put on the coat and boots. Each second I stayed in this house was another second wasted. He wouldn't stay upstairs forever.

Rushing to the kitchen, I grabbed a knife from the butcher block then reached for the bag. The island was empty. I looked at the floor around it, thinking one of the infected might have knocked the bag off. Nope. It wasn't there either.

"Did you think I wouldn't know you'd try to run again?" Ghua asked from behind me.

I cringed and turned slowly. He held the packed bag in front of him, using it as a shield since he was still naked. Light glinted off his wet chest and hard abs.

I met his unwavering gaze.

"What did you expect after you danced around naked in front of me?"

"I did not dance. I stood still."

"You're still naked."

He grunted in that increasingly familiar way. I was starting to think it was his way of acknowledging I was right without saying it.

He glanced at the knife in my hand and tilted his head at me.

"Come back upstairs so I can find clothes and keep you safe."

I sighed, put the knife down, and made my way back upstairs.

While he searched for something to wear, I sat on the bed and ate some applesauce. After I finished, I closed myself in the bathroom to actually use it this time. I didn't hurry. Instead, I enjoyed washing my hands and using the toothbrush once more. Who knew when I'd next get the chance to clean up so well, again? I stuck the toothbrush and paste into the inner pocket of my coat then opened the door.

Ghua, fully dressed, waited near the bed. The sweatpants he'd found didn't quiet reach his anklebones and fit so tightly I knew he was hanging to the right. The shirt was just as tight.

"We need to find you some clothes that fit."

He grunted again. "Human men are smaller."

"Yeah, I guess so."

I looked around the room. It had been comfortable for the night, and I wished I could have something like that again permanently. My gaze lingered on the dresser. Hell, I'd settle for being able to change my underwear more than once a week. As much as I wanted that, I wasn't about to give up an ounce of food space for clothes in the bag Ghua shouldered.

"Are you ready, Eden?"

I nodded and followed him out the door. When he reached the porch, he stopped and looked down at me.

"It will be faster if I carry you."

In my peripheral, I caught his pants move. Even without directly looking, the outline of his package was more prominent than it had been a minute ago. Sweet baby Jesus. He liked the idea of carrying me far too much.

"You know what? After all that sleep, my legs are kind of itching to stretch out. I think I'll walk for a while."

I quickly stepped off the porch and headed north, the same general direction he'd followed yesterday. Ghua fell in step beside me, his soft buckskin boots making little noise on the dried lawn or the debris when we entered the trees.

While we walked, my mind replayed the morning. Waking,

snuggled and warm. Dongzilla swinging free between Ghua's legs. Ghua telling me to go hide in the bathroom so he could kill the infected. Ghua trying to shield Dongzilla from my eyes. Ghua finding me in the kitchen and not getting mad.

I glanced over at him. He immediately met my gaze.

"Are you tired? I can carry you."

I shook my head and focused on the forest floor. He wasn't going to kill me. That much seemed clear. I was far from comforted by the revelation, though, because Van had made that clear, too. Why was it so impossible to just be left alone? I didn't want to sleep with either of them in exchange for safety. Yet, it seemed like I might not get a choice. If I ran from Ghua, where would I go? Straight back to Van? I seemed damned either way.

"Are you angry because you saw me naked? Timmy never looks. I did not know you would."

"What? No, I'm not angry you were naked. Why do you think I'm angry?"

"You are walking hard and making more noise." He pulled the pack off his shoulder and reached into one of the side compartments. The last thing I expected to see was the knife from the kitchen, which he held out to me.

"Would it make you feel better to carry this?"

I hesitantly took the knife from him. In all the weeks I'd been locked in the bunker with Oscar's crew, never once had they let me close to any type of real weapon to carry. Ghua hadn't been any different. He'd taken every weapon I'd found away from me until this moment. Why give me one now?

"Put it in your pocket so you do not fall on it. If you cut yourself, I will take it away."

Tearing my gaze from the long, wicked blade, I looked up at

the big grey man beside me. Was this a test? Was he waiting for me to lash out at him? I wasn't that stupid.

"Thank you. This does make me feel better."

He grinned, showing his pointed teeth.

"You are welcome, Eden. We will find you more if you are careful with that one."

I doubted he'd ever allow me more but didn't say so.

With my knife in hand, I walked beside him in silence once more. We stopped in the trees for a quiet lunch of canned tuna. He wouldn't eat until I started eating first; and when I finished my can, he immediately offered me another one.

"We need to ration our food," I said. "One can a day is enough."

"No. Two cans a meal. Three times a day. I will get more cans when these are gone."

"If you haven't noticed, it's not easy to find food."

He studied me for a moment. "It's not easy for you to find food. It is easy for me, though."

His message was clear. *Stick with me, and I'll feed you like a queen.* No thanks.

A distant shot rang out, echoing in the woods. Ghua turned his head and looked to the east. A quick volley of shots followed the first. Ghua put the can he'd been trying to give me back into the bag then stood.

"Come, Eden, we must go see what that is."

He impatiently held out his hand. I mutinously crossed my arms and stayed sitting.

"That is trouble. We don't want to go toward it; we want to go away from it. That kind of noise will draw every infected in the area."

He glanced to the east again then back down at me.

"There might be humans who need help. Females."

I knew it.

"So you're willing to risk me to get more females for your collection? Nice to know where I stand."

He frowned. "I will not risk you."

"Yes, you will if you take me to a gun fight with a stupid knife. Do you not remember the last guys who took me?"

He grunted and looked around.

"I cannot leave you here."

I quickly stood.

"Yes, you can."

He focused on me, the look in his yellow eyes way too intelligent. He knew I'd run as soon as he turned his back.

"I'm not letting you go, Eden. Ever. When are you going to understand that?"

I stomped my foot like the child he thought me to be.

"Maybe when you understand that's all I want from you. My freedom, not your overgrown meat stick."

He tilted his head. "Meat stick?"

"Never mind. I'm a kid. I don't know what I'm talking about."

"You understand more than I think, remember?"

I crossed my arms and looked away, pretending my heart wasn't racing a million miles per hour because of the shift in conversation.

He sighed gustily and stepped closer to me. I warily dropped my arms, ready to run or...I looked at the knife still lying on the ground. How could I have forgotten it?

Inches from me, Ghua curled his hands around my biceps and set his forehead to mine.

"There will come a time you no longer fear me. You will

look at me and smile and laugh."

"Don't bet on it," I said softly, my voice shaking.

He brushed his nose against mine and then said the last thing I expected to hear from his lips.

"Grab the branch."

I jerked back to look at him in shock, thinking he meant his dick. Before I could open my mouth to tell him to go to hell, he tossed me into the air.

My lungs froze. I couldn't scream. A branch whizzed past me. Then another. My ascent started to slow, and I knew what would happen next. Descent. Instinctively, I reached out for the next branch I saw. Pulling myself over, I fell on top of it with an "oof" and wrapped my arms and legs around its girth.

"Are you secure?" Ghua asked from below.

I lifted my head from the thick branch and looked down at him. My stomach pitched a bit at the distance, and I quickly focused on the branch once more.

"Are you insane? I could have hurt myself." I still could. I had to be at least twenty feet in the air. I had no idea what kind of tree this was, but there weren't many branches below me and none of them close to the ground. I'd never be able to climb down.

"I made sure you would miss the branches going up. If you didn't grab that one, I would have caught you and tried again."

"You would have thrown me a second time?" My sweaty palms slid against the cold, rough bark as I carefully eased myself upright enough to straddle the branch.

"Your heart is still beating fast."

"No shit! You threw me into a tree. Why?" My stomach twisted some more as I slowly scooted backward until my shoulder blades touched the trunk.

"The infected do not know how to climb. You will be safe up there while I go check the gunshots."

"You're leaving me?" I closed my eyes and took a calming breath before looking down at Ghua. It wasn't so bad now that I had my back to the tree to steady me.

"Only for a few minutes. Here."

He threw the backpack toward me. My eyes widened, and I tightened my thighs around the branch, anticipating the bag's weight and the downward pull of gravity. Ghua's throw, however, was perfect. The bag rose up just beside me, and I jerked it toward my chest.

"Stay in the tree, Eden." Warning laced those words.

"How do I know you'll come back?"

"Nothing can keep me from returning to you."

When I looked down, he was gone. I swore again and considered my options. The next branch was about five feet below me. Two feet below it was another one. But, even if I worked my way down to the bottom branch, it was still a long way down.

I had to try, right? I shifted the weight of the bag to the left, which off balanced me a little. I yipped, clutched the bag and shook my head. Nope. I didn't need to try. Not at all. I'd just stay in the damn tree until that big, grey pain-in-my-ass came back.

Gradually my heart stopped trying to beat its way out of my ribcage enough that I could think clearly and look around better. If I stayed in the tree, I would be wasting an opportunity I wouldn't likely get again. I needed to think of this tree like a porch roof. I'd dropped off of those plenty of times.

Keeping my eye on my current perch, I balanced the bag in front of me and pushed it out far enough so I wouldn't knock it down. When I did that, my palm touched something hard in the side compartment. Stunned, I dug out the knife I'd dropped on the ground. Was that Ghua's way of doubling up the protection? Putting me in a tree with a knife?

I shook my head and put the weapon back in the bag. I did not want to accidentally cut myself trying to get down.

It took a bit of work and slow breathing to turn myself so that I faced the trunk. More still, to get myself to the next branch. After collecting the bag from the branch above, I lowered myself to a sitting position against the trunk and took a break to allow the shaking to ease up a bit.

My stomach hurt from dangling off the branch above. My palms were red and full of splinters. And, I was pretty sure my chin was scraped raw. But I was alive and one step closer to the ground.

As I sat there, I watched the trees. Something moved in the distance. It darted in and out of the trees too fast to focus until it was almost right under me.

"Are you ready?" Ghua called.

"No, you jackass. Go away for another ten minutes."

"You will hurt yourself if you try to get down without me. And someone needs your help."

"Who? Another female? I'm not going to help you collect more, you pervert. Go away and leave me alone."

"You are wasting time. The gunshots were from an old man in a house not far from here. Something happened. Other men were there. I think they took the old man's food then left him there with too many infected. I killed the infected, but the old man is afraid of me. You need to talk to him. He will not survive long if he stays there alone.

"I can catch you or climb up to get you. Climbing will take

longer, and I'm not sure how safe the old man is. Choose, Eden."

I hung my head in defeat. Oh, I didn't give a crap about some old man stuck in his house. I just knew that getting down with or without help was going to suck.

"How do I know you'll catch me?"

"Because I've been wanting to hold you all day."

I looked down at him with a scowl.

"I'm a kid, remember?"

"I know. And you're afraid all of the time. That's why I want to comfort you."

Comfort, my ass.

I threw the bag at him. He caught it with ease and tossed it aside.

"Do you want me to get you?" he asked when I hesitated to move further.

"No. Just a minute." I crawled down to the next branch then dangled off the end. I looked down at him. He could almost touch my feet.

"Let go, Eden. I will keep you safe."

I let go. Arms immediately encircled me, guiding my descent. When my feet touched the ground, I sagged with relief and set my head against his chest. His arms stayed around me, and he held me until my shaking stopped. It wasn't until then that I noticed he wasn't wearing a shirt. My hands were gripping his bare arms.

"Please tell me you're wearing pants," I whispered.

"Of course."

I pushed away from him and saw he was telling the truth. The dirty sweats still didn't leave anything to the imagination, though.

He clapped his hands in front of my face.

"Eden, look at my eyes. Up here, not down there."

My mouth dropped open as I looked up at him.

He grunted, turned away, and picked up the bag. Then, without giving me an option, scooped me up into his arms.

"When you are eighteen, I will let you look some more."

Nine

Ghua took off running, the rush of wind robbing me of breath and forcing me to take cover in the shelter of his shoulder. Not that I really wanted to press my face against his bare chest with his words still ringing in my ears. Did he honestly think I wanted to look at him more? The image of Dongzilla was already burned into my brain.

Just as quickly as the buffeting wind started, it stopped. I lifted my head and looked around.

We stood at the edge of the trees beside a garage. Across the driveway, a white two-story house looked like it had endured a war. Bullet holes riddled the siding. Jagged panes of glass partially filled most of the front windows. The ones by the front door had no glass at all.

The barrel of a shotgun suddenly protruded from one of those windows.

"Get the hell off my property."

Ghua growled, turned, and set me on my feet.

"Stay here," he said.

Before I could turn toward him or the house, the gun fired, and I dove for cover behind the garage.

"Shooting hurts," Ghua yelled a moment before I heard something crash.

I peeked around the side of the building in time to see the

gun go flying out the window.

"Eden is here to talk to you since you do not like me. You will not hurt her."

Ghua strode from the broken front door a moment later. I stood up and glanced at the trees, wanting to kick myself for not immediately running.

"No, Eden," Ghua said softly, his voice sounding much too close.

When I looked back, he was only feet from me. He didn't say anything, just held out his hand. I crossed my arms, refusing to touch him, and started toward the house. I only made it a step past him when he swept me into his arms.

I glared up at him.

"I can walk."

"Yes, but if he has more guns, I can run faster."

He had me there.

Ghua walked right up to the house and stepped inside. An older man stood in the dated sitting room. The pallor of his skin and tremble in his hands sent a tiny bit of pity welling up inside of me. I knew what he was feeling. It seemed a pretty reasonable response after seeing Ghua for the first time, having him take a gun away, and getting scolded for shooting it. I was surprised the man was still standing.

"You might want to sit for a minute," I said, "until the shock passes."

The man didn't move.

"My name's Eden. This is Ghua. He took me a few days ago."

"I saved you, Eden. I killed the infected and stopped the men from taking you, and I untied you."

Something about Ghua's words had the man focusing on

me.

"Men?" he asked.

"Yeah. There's a group further south of here. They found a bunker and have been rounding up survivors to use as workers."

"Just met them. They're the ones who busted up my house. They took all my food after they shot out the windows. Didn't take me because I'm too old to live long. Their words. Not mine."

My stomach sank at hearing that. The gunmen shouldn't have been here. They'd said they had enough supplies and were ready to hole up for the winter. That meant Oscar and Van were still looking for me.

"Come with us," Ghua said.

A groan came from outside the house. Ghua set me on my feet.

"Do not hurt Eden," he warned the old man. He looked at me. "Stay here." Then, he disappeared out the front door.

"Do you have any other guns?" I hurriedly asked the old man.

He shook his head, and I swore. Through the busted window, I watched Ghua grapple with an infected who'd wandered into the yard.

"Listen, he thinks I'm a kid," I said softly. "It's the only thing keeping me from being his sex toy. Please don't say anything."

The man nodded and answered just as quietly. "Won't say a thing."

The infected made a loud sound then everything fell silent. Covered in fresh infected blood, Ghua came back inside.

"Come," Ghua said to the old man. "You cannot stay here. It's not safe."

The old guy shook his head. "I'm staying."

Ghua looked at me, and I shrugged. I had no idea why he thought I'd want to talk the guy into agreeing to leave with us. I didn't even want to be with us.

"Familiar places give people a sense of safety, even if that safety is just an illusion. If he doesn't want to go, he doesn't want to go," I said.

Ghua sighed and looked at all the broken windows.

"Do you have a hammer, nails, and wood to board the windows up?" he asked the man.

My mouth dropped open. I'd thought the man's fate would be similar to mine, taken without being given a choice in the matter.

"You're going to let him stay?" I asked.

"I will not force him if he does not want to leave."

"What about me? You're forcing me."

"You are a child and a female. You need protection."

"I have nails and wood and such in the garage," the old man said, shuffling in the direction of the kitchen. He grabbed the garage door opener off the top of the fridge and tossed it to Ghua, who caught it with ease.

Ghua's gaze shifted to me.

"Come, Eden. You can help."

"Nah, I'll clean up the broken glass in here," I said, thinking quickly.

"No, Eden. You will try to leave. Come."

"How come you're not worried about him leaving?"

"Because he wants to stay."

Annoyed that Ghua wasn't giving me any chance to run, I had no choice but to follow him outside. When we got to the garage, though, he moved to break in the side door.

"Wait! We might need that door. Push the button on the

thing you're holding." He looked down at the opener, pushed the large button, then grinned widely as the bay door started to rise.

Within five minutes, I understood why he'd wanted me to help him. The garage door wasn't the only thing he had no idea about. He understood the use of a hammer, nails, screwdriver, and screws, but he had no idea how to take a door off its hinges or why caulk was useful.

"If we're going to use these sheets of plywood to board the broken windows, it makes sense to caulk them so the cold air doesn't get in." After I said that, I wondered why it even mattered. Sure, I'd do it if I was fixing and sealing up my own place, but I didn't see the old man having much of a chance on his own.

Ghua grunted and added the caulk to the items we'd gathered in the bucket. While he carried out the sheets of wood, I hauled the other supplies to the front of the house.

Fifteen minutes later, Ghua hand sawed a sheet to fit the first window, using the lines I'd measured and drawn as a guide. I watched him for a moment, unable to believe how quickly he was tearing through the material.

"How do you know some of this stuff?" I asked.

"Dad taught us when we started putting solar panels on our houses. He said that a man needs to know how to be handy." He finished cutting and looked up at me. "You're handy too, Eden."

"Thanks." I didn't want to be handy. I wanted to be free.

He watched me apply a bead of caulk then took the board to the window and screwed it securely to the frame in seconds.

We quietly worked together for several hours. Any time I even glanced at the woods, Ghua was right there to tell me it wasn't safe. The infected that kept wandering into the yard and the seven bodies stacked behind the garage proved his point.

While we made progress on the first story, I listened to the old man clean up inside. He made several trips to empty the glass shards onto the driveway leading up to the house. I grinned at his cleverness. If the gunmen returned, they'd hopefully get a set of flat tires for their troubles.

By the time the sun dipped behind the trees, we had the first floor secured.

"Eden, go inside," Ghua said. "I will put these things away."

Of course he'll let me stay inside on my own now, I thought. We'd just spent the last several hours sealing up all potential exits.

With zero enthusiasm, I shuffled inside.

"Do you mind if I use your bathroom?" I asked the man.

"No. Go ahead. You two ready to leave?"

I looked outside. "I think he's going to want to stay here tonight. Sorry."

Moving down the hall, I found the bathroom and turned on the light. With the windows boarded, the old man would need to keep the lights on all the time if he wanted to see anything. Not necessarily a bad thing given what was likely to come out at night.

After using the toilet and washing my hands, I headed back to the kitchen.

"Are you hungry?" I asked. "We have some canned goods."

I grabbed the bag by the door, only slightly surprised the guy hadn't already checked it. By the time we had three cans of soup heated, Ghua came in and closed the newly constructed front door.

"Eat, Eden," he said when he caught me looking at him.

The infected blood he'd ended up wearing throughout the day had acted like glue for the sawdust he'd created. Instead of looking grey-skinned, he almost looked human-colored, if a person could ignore the tarred and feathered texture.

I forced my gaze away from him and started sipping my soup. The old man handed Ghua his share then started eating his own.

"How is it that the infected haven't broken into this place yet?" I asked between swallows.

"Once I figured out the light that was keeping the hounds away was drawing the infected, I stopped leaving the lights on down here and blocked the windows upstairs."

"The infected are drawn to light?" I asked, stunned. No wonder I'd been having problems.

"Yep. For at least two weeks now. If I," he stumbled over that word, "keep quiet, the hounds don't come close either."

Ghua, who'd been quietly eating while listening to our conversation, suddenly spoke up.

"Come, Eden. I need to shower."

I choked on my soup.

"I don't want to see that again."

He frowned at me. "No. You shouldn't. But you need to be upstairs where I can listen to you."

I heaved a sigh and finished my soup. While the old man ran water to wash our cups, Ghua took my hand and started leading me upstairs.

"Wait," the man called. "There's a shower down here."

"Is there one upstairs?" Ghua asked, pausing.

The man paled as he nodded.

"It is easier to listen to Eden upstairs."

"That makes no sense," I said.

Ghua's gaze pinned me.

"I will hear you on the stairs if you try to leave."

I rolled my eyes at him and said nothing when he started tugging me forward again. The old man hurried after us to the second floor. It wasn't a big second story. Because of the pitched roof, the rooms were small with slanted ceilings. The first one fit a full-sized bed. There were pictures on the dresser, a display of black and whites with a few modern ones thrown in.

"Is this your room?" Ghua asked.

"Yes," the man answered. I didn't miss the quaver in his voice.

Ghua continued down the hall and looked into the door of a cramped upstairs bathroom.

"Here, let me get you a towel," the man said, opening the hall closet located directly across from the bathroom.

"Thank you," Ghua said without waiting for it.

He pulled me past the bathroom and stepped into the final room, a small space done in pale pink. Boy band and movie star posters plastered the slanted ceiling over the neatly made twin bed.

"Eden, you wait in here." Ghua gave me a firm stare. "No looking this time."

"I didn't want to look last time."

The skepticism on his face made me want to throw a punch. I knew better though.

"Do you have clean clothes that will fit me?" Ghua asked the man when he came into the room, carrying a towel.

The old guy nodded and motioned for Ghua to follow him.

"I have something from my son-in-law in my closet that might fit."

The way the man hurried away from the pink room struck

me as odd, but I didn't dwell on it when Ghua turned to me.

"Stay, Eden."

"I'm not a damn dog."

"No swearing."

I kept my mouth shut and glared at him. He grunted and followed the old man. I looked at the room and tried not to let regret swamp me. A little girl had slept there not too long ago. How many people had died? How many still lived who had to deal with the loss?

The water started, and from the sound of it, Ghua hadn't shut the door.

I shook my head and moved toward the dresser. Like the old man's dresser, it had pictures displayed. I picked one up.

"My daughter and her husband," the old man said from the doorway. "And my granddaughter."

I glanced at him then did a double-take. Sweat was starting to bead on his forehead. Why? He hadn't been sweating before. Not even when he first saw Ghua.

The old man's gaze flicked to the stubby attic door under the eaves.

My heart sank as I once more took in the girly, dust free room and all the pictures of his daughter and son-in-law. They didn't age past the picture I held.

"How long ago was this picture taken?" I asked, looking at the infant.

"Twelve years."

I nodded and set the picture down.

"What happened to your daughter and son-in-law?"

"Car accident."

He was starting to shake.

"How long ago?"

"Eleven years."

I nodded again and set the picture down. The water shut off causing the old man to look at the attic door once more.

"What's your name?" I asked.

"Benjamin."

Ghua walked into the room. He wore a pair of athletic shorts, and that was it. At least they weren't skin tight.

"Thank you for the shorts, Benjamin. It is getting dark. You should lay down, Eden." He moved toward the bed to pull back the covers.

Benjamin looked ready to faint.

"Can we use your room, instead?" I asked.

"Yes, of course," Benjamin said.

"Eden, we are not supposed to take other people's things."

"No, no! I don't mind at all," Benjamin hurried to assure Ghua.

"No. It is not kind."

"We both won't fit on that bed, Ghua," I said, hating myself on so many different levels.

I did not want to sleep in the same bed with him. Not after what happened that morning. I also didn't want to use his name. He was already starting to seem way too human to me the way it was. But, I didn't see how I had much of a choice. I needed to do something to get him out of the room.

I wasn't being altruistic or anything. If Ghua knew there was a girl hiding in the attic, he'd insist on taking her with. He'd been pretty clear about the whole children and females don't get a choice thing. Keeping silent wasn't to save the girl from the same unknown fate I faced. It was to keep me safe just a little longer. Because, if there was a twelve-year-old girl hiding in that attic, Ghua was bound to notice we didn't look the same, and I feared what he would do if he found out I'd been lying.

"You said I sleep better when you're by me," I added.

He moved closer to me and pulled me into his arms. His large hand stroked over my hair, just missing the lump I still had on my head from Ty's gun.

"I will keep you safe, Eden."

"Yeah," I said with a sigh. "I know."

"I insist you take my room," Benjamin said. "You're my guests, and it's the least I can do after you've helped me so much today."

"Thank you," Ghua said. He threaded his fingers through mine and started leading me from the room.

I hesitated at the doorway.

"I've never zombie-proofed a house before. Just in case the wood downstairs doesn't hold, you might want to close the door. I wouldn't blame you if you even wanted to move the dresser in front of it. Try not to make noise after the sun sets, though."

Benjamin nodded in gratitude as I left the room with Ghua.

I didn't feel very gracious when Ghua closed the door behind us, trapping me in yet another bedroom with him. He strode over to the bed and pulled back the sheets. When I moved to get in, he stopped me.

"Jacket and shoes off."

"What if an infected comes in, and I need to run?"

"I will keep you safe, Eden. Take them off. You'll sleep better."

My ass I'd sleep better, I thought. He just wanted to make sure I wouldn't try to sneak away. The determined look in Ghua's eyes kept me from arguing, though.

With a scowl, I did as he wanted then tried to ignore him as I crawled under the covers. It proved impossible because he got in right behind me.

I rolled away from him, thinking he'd take the hint and leave me alone. Nope. He took it as an invitation to spoon me again.

His large arm snaked around my waist and pulled me back against the solid wall of his chest. Heat radiated from him, a reminder of his barely clothed state.

"Why can't you sleep on top of the covers?"

"Because I wouldn't be able to hold you like this while you sleep."

"Good, because I don't like this."

"You don't like anything."

Sighing gustily, he relaxed behind me. Each exhale tickled my ear.

I closed my eyes and tried to force myself to sleep. It wasn't easy. I couldn't stop picturing Ghua trying to cover the equipment that was now resting peacefully against my backside. I inched my hips forward a little, breaking the contact.

He made a disgruntled sound and snuggled close again. This time, I was sure I could feel…it.

"Go to sleep, Eden," Ghua said with impatience, like I was being the difficult one.

I rolled over so I was facing him. Inches from his face, I shot him a glare.

"I can't with your penis touching my butt."

He frowned.

"You should not want it touching your front either. Close your eyes and sleep, my Eden, and stop thinking about my penis. It makes me uncomfortable."

I sputtered, unable to come up with anything to say that wouldn't somehow get turned back around to me.

His lips brushed my forehead, and his fingers began to

stroke through my hair. Despite everything I'd gone through, I found both gestures comforting and closed my eyes in defeat.

Ten

I yawned, my jaw cracking with the enormity of it, and let myself drift between awake and asleep. Fingers ran through my hair, and I snuggled closer to my personal heater. I knew exactly where I was and who I snuggled. I was just too comfortable to care.

After giving into cuddle time the night before, I'd gotten the best night's sleep I could remember since seeing the first infected shuffle past my bedroom window. However, it wasn't a sign of me giving up. It was just me acknowledging that, sometimes, I needed to take each moment as it came. I had nowhere to go because Ghua wouldn't let me, and I was safe enough to get as much sleep as I wanted.

A door further down the hall opened and closed. Then, footsteps echoed outside our door.

Ghua slipped out from under me—I'd been partially using him as a body pillow—and quietly left the room. His exit dispelled any hint of remaining sleepiness. I opened my eyes and quickly got out of bed, taking a moment to peel back the paper from the window. The clear blue sky and the amount of daylight almost blinded me.

I embraced the new moment and dashed for my boots and jacket. Holding both, I opened the door and almost screamed. Ghua stood within the frame, leaning against the side.

His gaze swept me from head to toe, lingering on what I held.

"Yeah, yeah," I said. "Do not go outside, Eden. I'll keep you safe, Eden. Hold still so I can butthump you, Eden," I mimicked using a low tone. "I get it; you're in charge." I dropped my things and crossed my arms in a real pout. "Do I still get breakfast?"

"Of course." He straightened away from the door and motioned for me to go downstairs.

I did while thinking all sorts of vile thoughts about Ghua. Damn guy had eyes in the back of his head.

"I did not have sex with you with my butt," he said when we reached the bottom.

I stopped walking.

"What?"

"I did not butthump you."

I scrubbed my hands over my face. "Okay. Fine. Just forget I said it. Now, if it's all right with you, I'd like to use the bathroom."

He grunted, which I took as a yes. When I turned to go down the hall, I found Benjamin watching us from the kitchen. I didn't say anything, just continued on my way.

Through the bathroom door, I heard the deep rumble of Ghua's voice.

"Can I ask you a question, Benjamin?"

"Sure."

"Why does Eden always seem so angry with me? Are twelve-year-olds always like that?"

I held my breath, waiting for the answer.

"Most people don't like being kidnapped, no matter what their age."

"I didn't kidnap her."

"She sees it that way."

After Ghua's non-committal grunt, they didn't speak again, and I hurried to use the bathroom.

The smell of frying spam teased my nose as I opened the door, and my stomach growled. Ghua sat at the kitchen table, watching Ben move around the kitchen until I entered the room.

"Did you brush your teeth, Eden?" he asked.

"No, you stole my jacket so I didn't have my toothbrush."

He nodded and stood. "Stay here, Eden. I will get your toothbrush for you."

I watched him leave the room and glanced at Ben. The old man watched me, probably wondering what I'd do. Make a run for it? I wanted to. But, I hesitated to just go bolting out the door with all the windows boarded up. I had no idea what was lurking out there.

Not that I had any real choice in the matter because Ghua returned a few short seconds later with my boots and coat. I took the coat from him, dug my toothbrush and paste from the pocket, then went to brush my teeth. Personal grooming two days in a row and a good night's sleep? Yep, I was getting spoiled.

The next time I joined them, a plate lay on the table for me. The plate before Ghua was already empty while Ben toyed with his portion. Ignoring them both, I sat and started eating my peas and spam.

"Did the men from yesterday say anything about where they were headed?" I asked between bites.

"No. They just asked if there was anyone else here, took what supplies I had, and left. You two leaving today?"

"Yes," Ghua said. "I must return home." He sounded a little

troubled when he said that. When I looked up from my food, I caught him watching me with a peculiar expression. As soon as our eyes met, he focused on Benjamin.

"We will leave our food here for you. Do you have any more clothes that would fit me?"

"Wait, what?" I said. I didn't mind sharing but completely giving it all away? Hell, no.

"Food isn't easy to find, Ghua, and I don't like starving."

"Food isn't easy for humans to find, but I have no problem finding it. You will not go hungry."

"I have a box of Mike's old things in the basement. I'll go get them," Ben said.

He left his plate on the table. I forked up his portion of spam, completely unrepentant. No matter what Ghua said, I doubted we'd find more food today.

When Benjamin returned, he and Ghua went through the clothes. Canned goods were swapped out for six shirts and two pair of pants.

Not more than an hour after waking, we headed out the front door. I scanned the clear yard in a disgruntled mood. I should have run for it. Looking back, I believed I saw the same thought echoed in Benjamin's eyes.

"Take care of yourself, Eden," he said from the porch.

"You too. Don't stay here after we're gone. Find somewhere safer."

He closed the door, and I found myself once again alone with Ghua.

"Still north?" I asked, already taking steps in that direction.

"Yes."

"Figured."

"I must go there to tell my friends I will not live with them anymore."

That didn't sound good for my future.

"Why?" I asked.

"Because you do not want to live there. You can choose where we live."

He wasn't making any sense to me.

"Why do you want me to choose?"

"So you do not feel kidnapped anymore."

I snorted.

"Letting me choose the location of my imprisonment doesn't change the fact that I'm still your captive."

"But you are not my captive. I am yours."

I shot him an annoyed look.

"Yeah, right. I'm not sure you understand the meaning of captive."

"It means someone is not free to leave. That is what I am. I am not free to leave you, Eden. Where you go, I will go."

I studied his serious expression for a moment.

"You're telling me that if I decided to just start walking to the east you wouldn't try to stop me?"

"If there's danger, I will stop you to protect you."

A convenient out since everything was dangerous nowadays. Just to test him, I turned to the east and started walking. He moved with me without commenting or trying to stop me. Not that his silence convinced me. It wasn't like we'd veered very far yet. He'd put a stop to it before too long.

However, after an hour walking to the east, I began to wonder if he actually believed everything he had said.

"So, this place to the north that you wanted to take me. What's it like?"

"It's a good place with many houses. We built a wall around

them to keep the infected and hounds out. The hounds still try to get in, but the infected leave us alone. They are smarter now and know we kill them. They don't want to die, so they stay away."

"That sounds terrifying. That they've gotten that smart," I clarified at his confused look. "The houses sound great."

"They are. They have electricity from the solar panels Dad helped us install. And each house has its own well. That means they all have running water, too. It is a nice place. Much different from the caves we lived in, but I like the sun."

"You lived in caves?"

"Yes, for thousands of years. Thousands of years of nothing but darkness and the hounds trying to get inside our walls. It is not a life I want for you, Eden. If you do not want to live inside the walls we have made here, I understand."

"It's not the walls that I'm protesting," I said. "It's the loss of freedom. Walls sound like a great idea."

"What freedom would you lose?" he asked.

"Are you serious? You pretty much told me when I'm eighteen I'm going to be your sex slave. What if I don't want to have sex with you?"

He studied the trees around us.

"I'm not supposed to talk about this with children. Mya and Mom both said—"

"They aren't here. I am. And the idea of you waiting for me to be old enough to have sex with you is terrifying."

He scratched the end of his long ear, and I noticed how dark the grey was getting. Was he blushing?

"Eden, I will be your friend and protect you always. It does not matter if you never see me as something more. I will not abandon you."

I could feel my disbelief waver just a tiny bit before it firmed again. No one was that nice. Everyone wanted something. It was like that even before the world went to shit, and I was sure Ghua was no different than humans in that regard. He might not want anything from me now, but that would change when he learned how old I really was.

"We'll see," I said instead of arguing.

We walked in silence for another few minutes before he put out a hand and stopped me. Without the soft sound of our passing, I could hear the faint call of an infected.

"We should go around," he said softly.

"Infected are usually around houses or other people. Both are likely to have food."

He grunted and looked toward the east, the direction we were heading, then up at the nearest tree.

"No," I said firmly. "I am not spending more time stuck in a tree."

"I can't take you with me because you could get hurt. I can't leave you because you will try to leave. What would you have me do?"

"We don't even know what's ahead. If we get into a sticky spot, then you can throw me into a tree."

Tree tossing turned out to be unnecessary. After ten more minutes of walking, we found a house with two infected shambling around it. Ghua quickly ended the man and woman, and I waited outside while he checked the house.

"It is safe," he said, returning to the door.

I went inside and started looking through the cabinets and the freezer. Everything was empty except for the low cabinet right behind two dishes set on the floor. I opened the door and found twelve cans of dog food.

"We'll eat well tonight." I started taking the cans out and passing them back to Ghua.

"Mya said we aren't supposed to eat the ones that have pictures of dogs or cats."

"Mya obviously hasn't gone without food for a few days or she wouldn't be so picky. Read the ingredients. It's no worse than a can of spam or jar of wieners."

"I can't read."

I glanced up at him. "Really?"

He nodded.

"Then you'll just need to trust me. It's not so bad, and it'll keep your belly full."

I popped the lid off of one, and my stomach growled at the meaty smell. A quick search of the drawers produced two spoons.

"Give it a try," I said, scooping some out for him. He took the spoon but didn't eat his bite.

"Chicken?"

He frowned and glanced at the brown glop on his spoon.

"No, it is dog food."

"I know. I meant are you afraid to eat it?"

"No. I am waiting for you to eat first. The strongest eats first."

"You think I'm strong?"

He reached out and touched my hair, which I'd pulled back into a ponytail.

"Your hair is longer than mine. It shows you have not died. You're very strong."

"Huh. Alrighty then." I dipped my spoon in and took a healthy bite.

The one thing about dog food was that it wasn't nearly as

salty as people food. Still tasted pretty good, though.

Ghua took his bite, and his eyes widened in surprise.

"This is good."

I grinned when he reached for his own can and popped the lid off.

"I'd rather have people food over dog food," I said, watching him dig in. "But, dog food beats starvation."

I wandered around the kitchen and living room as I ate, and my gaze caught the cloudy haze of the kitchen window. A tap on the pane confirmed it wasn't glass but a hard, thick kind of plastic. Harder to break. A few of the other windows on the first floor had been swapped out, too. I wondered how many times the infected had tried to break their way into the house before they'd finally succeeded in getting the owners.

Checking the faucets, I discovered that the water ran in the kitchen. The hall light turned on and off, too.

"We should stay here for the night," he said. "We might not find another house with water and electricity before night falls."

I shrugged. "Sure."

I continued my exploration of the house, looking for anything useable. In one of the upstairs bedrooms, I found better clothes for myself. Sturdy jeans and a warm, long-sleeved shirt to layer under my hoodie. And, while searching through a bedroom closet, I found a bigger bag.

"We should use this one instead of the one we have," I said tossing it to Ghua. "It has room for everything in our current bag, the cans downstairs, and more supplies if we find another stocked house tomorrow."

He grunted and inspected the bag.

"You know, we'll have even more room if you ditch the dirty clothes you have on now and put on something clean."

He tore his gaze from the bag and frowned at me. "You may not see my penis again."

My mouth dropped open for a moment before I recovered. "What? Why would you even think that's what I meant?"

He continued to look at me with suspicion.

"Just go take a shower and come out dressed. Please."

"I can't. Not until the sun is almost down."

"Why?"

"You will run."

"Fine. You know what? I'm going to take a shower, then."

I set clean clothes aside for the next day and grabbed some sleep shorts, a tank top, and a t-shirt to help hide my boobs. If he was going to watch me like a hawk so I couldn't run, then I was going to use that to my benefit. He'd proven he could keep me safe, and I wanted to feel normal for just one night. Four days ago, it would have been a crazy risk. It probably still was now but for different reasons. It didn't matter. I was determined to grab another night of good sleep.

"Enjoy your guard duty." I closed myself in the bathroom and dug through the supplies the prior owners had left behind.

While the daylight faded, I soaked in a bathtub full of hot water. It was amazing. I washed and shaved. The razor looked like I'd attacked a mouse rather than myself when I finished. I didn't suffer an ounce of self-disgust, though. I'd been through too much to waste time with that.

By the time I drained the water, I felt completely clean and relaxed. My hands even looked unstained and dirt free. A first in weeks.

I dried, put on my pajamas, and opened the bathroom door to let out the steam since I'd purposely not used the fan.

Ghua stood out in the hall, waiting his turn. He'd ditched his shirt but had kept his pants on.

"It's all warmed up for you," I said, moving past him.

He grunted and stepped into the bathroom.

"The door stays open."

"Yeah, yeah. And no looking. I got it."

He grunted again, and I continued toward the bedroom after a quick glance at the blocked hallway. Even though the sun was only twenty minutes from setting, a little part of my mind whispered that I should at least try to run. I shut up that part with a little reminder that there were hellhounds out there. Plus, I did not want Ghua running after me naked. Ever.

Shaking my head at myself, I went to stand in front of the window and stared at the bright orange and red sunset. It was beautiful, familiar, and sad. How many of these had I missed since everything happened? How many more would I get to see? That was a question I couldn't avoid thinking about any longer.

Caged in the bunker, only let out for a few hours a day, I hadn't known just how much the infected had continued to evolve. That they were attracted to light now, the only thing that kept the hounds away at night, terrified me. What chance did I have to survive out here on my own? None. And it killed me to admit it. Where did that leave me then?

The water turned off in the bathroom.

In that moment, I acknowledged that staying with Ghua was an option. One I didn't like, but it was still there. But, so was crawling back to the bunker. I sighed and thought of the old man we'd just left. Returning to Benjamin's place wouldn't do me any good. He had no food, no gun, and a granddaughter to protect.

The future was bleak and not just for me.

A rustle of sound told me I wasn't alone. Before I could turn, fingers swiped over my hair followed by a brush. Gently,

Ghua began working the tangles from the wet strands. The third stroke went over the lump on my head. Ghua immediately stopped.

"Did I hurt you?" he asked.

"No. It's just a bump from before. It's almost gone, now. Just a little tender."

His fingers gently probed the spot. He grunted after a moment then resumed brushing, careful to avoid the fading bruise. The brush rasped against my scalp; and I closed my eyes, enjoying the feel while I considered my options.

I didn't like any of my choices. I wanted to be defiant and keep choosing option D, which was to go off on my own. At what cost? I hated the idea of compromising with my ideals even a little. I didn't want to end up like May, trading favors for protection. Yet, whether I wanted to admit it or not, Ghua was my most viable option for staying alive at present. And, he seemed to actually care. It was the caring that worried me, though.

"What would you do if I took my shirt off right now?"

"I would tell you it's too cold for a human to sleep without one."

When the brush swiped free on the next stroke, I stepped away from Ghua.

"Eden," he said in a chiding, impatient tone.

If I was thinking about staying, I had to know what I'd be compromising. With my resolve set, I gripped the bottoms of my shirts and pulled them off as I turned.

Ghua's eyes went wide, and his mouth dropped open. Wearing an expression of panic, he looked at the ceiling, the floor, the door, then back to me. A sound wheezed from him a second before he slapped his hands over his face. The bristles of the brush he obviously forgot he was holding stabbed him in the eye.

I cringed as he hissed in pain and dropped the thing. Had the sight of my boobs actually just blinded the one guy who could keep me safe?

Eleven

"Eden," Ghua said in a strangled voice, "put your shirt on, now. Peekaboo with boobs is a bad game."

I grabbed my t-shirt, tugged it over my head, and hurried to stop Ghua, who was slowly stumbling back toward the door.

"Are you okay?" I asked.

"No. Put your shirt on."

"It's on. Let me look at your face. Can you still see?"

He cautiously lowered his hands and relaxed slightly as he blinked his profusely watering eyes at me. He looked fine, physically, but I had the feeling I'd just mentally scarred him.

He grabbed me firmly by the shoulders.

"Boobs are private, Eden. Never let anyone see yours again."

I stared up into his watery gaze.

"Not even you once I'm eighteen?"

He swallowed visibly, released me, and brushed his hand over his mouth.

"No."

"What happens when I'm eighteen, and I take my shirt off again? Are you going to think that it means I want to have sex?" I pressed.

"No, Eden. I will keep my word. I will be your friend and keep you safe."

I desperately wanted to believe him.

Sighing, I picked up the brush and finished brushing my hair. Ghua said nothing as I crawled into bed and moved to the far side to make room for him. He surprised me by closing the door and sitting in front of it instead of joining me.

We stared at each other from across the room. Seeing him naked had upset me deeply, and I couldn't help but wonder if I'd just done the same to him.

"Did I scare you, Ghua?"

"Go to sleep, Eden."

I closed my eyes, and for the first time in forever, I went to sleep feeling safe, not just from the infected but Ghua too.

* * * *

The soft sound of Ghua's steady breathing tickled my awareness. I opened my eyes and found Ghua lying on top of the covers next to me. Weak, early morning light came in through the windows, proof that I'd lived through another night. Thanks, once more, to Ghua.

Unsure when he'd finally come to bed, I didn't move to get up. Curled on my side, I studied his sleep-relaxed face. His pointed ear rested against the pillow, partially buried in his long black hair. The darkness of him didn't seem so weird anymore, and that worried me. Anyone who was foolish enough to be lulled by anything these days ended up dead. Yet, I was so tired of fighting everything all the time.

If only I could trust what Ghua said. He'd proven so many times that I was safe with him. Now. When he thought me a child. How many times had I been burned by someone's smooth promises since the quakes, though?

Outside of Homer, a "family" that had supposedly stopped to help us when Dad was syphoning gas out of an abandoned pickup, convinced us that a bigger group was safer. They'd taken off with our supplies and vehicle in the middle of a scavenge run.

That was how my parents and I had ended up being taken by the first group of raiders. They'd promised to keep us safe with their guns while we searched houses. Only, their guns had been trained on us as often as they'd been trained on any infected. And, all that so-called protection hadn't kept my parents safe. When an infected bit Dad, he told me to run.

I'd escaped one group just to get snatched up by another. Oscar promised everyone equal shares for equal work. The food might have been equal, but the work hadn't been. And just like the rest, he'd wanted more than he'd said too.

Everyone lied. Everyone wanted more than what they said. Words were just used as smooth promises meant to hide darker intentions.

I gazed at Ghua and tried to ignore the hurt consuming my chest. I just wanted someone to be nice. To care. I wanted Ghua's offer of friendship to be genuine. I wasn't looking for a free ride, just a ride that wouldn't require me to lie on my back and spread my legs.

Unable to help myself, I shifted closer to Ghua and laid my head on his shoulder, soaking up the comfort of his nearness. His hand immediately smoothed over my head and down my back.

"Did you sleep well?" he asked, his voice a husky rumble, proving I'd just woken him.

"Yeah. Sorry for waking you up."

He turned his head toward me. The last thing I expected to feel was the warm brush of his lips against my forehead.

"It was time, anyway," he said. "Are you hungry?"

I nodded, trying to suppress my shock.

He rolled away from me and got out of bed in one fluid

move.

"I will pack the bag and leave a can of food out for you."

He left the room without looking at me. I lightly touched my forehead where his lips had pressed. My chest gave a weird squeeze, and I quickly rubbed the spot to erase the feel of the kiss.

Frowning, I got out of bed and quickly changed into the clean clothes I'd set out the night before. When I joined him downstairs, he had my coat and boots ready along with the can of food.

"There are a few infected outside. Stay in here and eat while I remove them."

Relieved he didn't mention the kiss, I slipped into my boots.

"I think you need to find a better way to kill," I commented. "Ripping off heads is way too messy. You'll run out of clean clothes at this rate, and your size isn't easy to find."

"How should I kill them?"

I shrugged and looked around the kitchen.

"I usually use a knife and stab them through their mouths. It works, but it's dangerous because they could bite."

"Their bites do not bother me." He pulled one of the knives out of the butcher block on the counter, then replaced it. "I might still get messy with a knife." He moved off to open the closet just off the kitchen and withdrew a mop.

"I will try killing them with this."

"A mop? That's for cleaning floors."

He grunted, already on his way toward the front door. I grabbed my food and rushed to the nearest window.

Each of the five infected stopped their listless shuffle and turned toward the sound of the door opening. Ghua stepped out onto the porch and gripped the end of the mop as the infected broke into a run. With a twist, Ghua removed the useless mop head, leaving behind a jagged metal end.

The first infected to reach Ghua got the mop handle shoved into its mouth so hard it erupted from the back of its head. With a jerk, Ghua freed his weapon while knocking back the second infected with his elbow. The woman stumbled back a step, giving Ghua enough room to twist around and skewer her the same as the first.

With lightning fast speed, he dislodged her then spun his weapon around to catch the next infected through the middle. It didn't kill the man, though. Ghua swung the mop to the side, sending the skewered man into the fourth infected. Both tumbled to the ground. Ignoring them, Ghua jabbed the metal end of the mop through the final infected to reach him. The two he'd knocked down never had a chance to get back to their feet before they joined the rest.

It had only taken him a minute, maybe two, to kill all of the infected. Stunned, I could only continue to stare as Ghua straightened, looked down at himself, then started toward the house. Not a spot of blood dotted his clothing.

"This works well," he said, coming inside.

He noticed me by the window and moved toward me.

"Where do you want to go today?"

How was it that the world could open up and offer so many more possibilities in just a span of a few seconds? I'd seen Ghua kill a single infected, and I'd witnessed the aftermath to know that he could kill many of them. But, until I'd seen it, I would never have believed the level of his abilities. I now understood his certainty that he could not only keep me safe but have an easier time finding food than me.

"I'm not sure," I answered. "But, I'm ready to get going."

"You didn't eat your breakfast yet."

"I'll eat while we walk."

The brisk morning air made my nose cold within minutes as we made our way further east. I had no idea where I was going. I was still just seeing how long he'd let me keep walking to the east. If we hit the ocean, perfect. I'd find a nice mansion on the beach to take over.

When I finished my can of food, I tossed it aside but pocketed the spoon.

"Would you like me to carry you?" Ghua asked.

He already had the backpack and mop weapon weighing him down.

"Nah, I think your hands are full enough."

"Did you remember to brush your teeth when you went to the bathroom?" he asked, treating me like the kid he thought me to be.

"Yep." I patted the pocket that held the toothbrush. "I can still taste the mint around the dog food."

He grunted and turned his head to the south.

"What is it?" I asked softly when his pace slowed.

"It sounds like a vehicle."

Without warning, he picked me up and started running.

"Are we running toward the sound or away?" I asked, still unable to hear what he'd heard.

"I'm keeping pace. I want to see where it goes."

The "where" turned out to be a subdivision on the outskirts of a small town. Ghua stopped before we reached the first house.

"I want you to wait in a tree," he said, setting me on my feet and taking off the bag.

"No way. I hated being up there."

"It kept you safe."

"It also trapped me. I would have killed myself trying to get down on my own if, for some reason, you never came back for me."

He grabbed the back of my head and pulled me in close to press his forehead against mine.

"I will always come back for you."

I shook my head in frustration. Just because he couldn't get infected didn't mean he couldn't die. The thought brought me up short.

"When you said you lived in caves for thousands of years, you meant your people, not you, right?"

"Both. My brothers and I have lived many lives in darkness. Why?"

"Does that mean you can't die?"

"In Ernisi, our old home, we never aged; and we never truly died. We were reborn."

"And up here?"

"Here we can truly die."

"This is not making me feel better," I whispered.

He pulled back to brush his lips against my forehead again.

"I will be back, my Eden."

Then, the rat bastard threw me into a tree again.

"You better hurry up," I whispered down to him. He nodded and ran toward the houses at the same time gunshots rang out.

Guns meant people. And, possibly the same caliber of people like the gunmen from the bunker. They'd shoot holes in Ghua without hesitation.

I looked at the ground and swore. My chances of making it down safely were slim. Ghua had, yet again, picked a tree where the lowest branch was at least eight feet off the ground.

The faint echo of someone's anguished cry reached my ears, and I frowned. Gunshots were bad. Yelling was worse. Whatever was happening couldn't be good.

Using the monkey skills I'd learned from my last stint in a tree, I worked my way down to the lowest branch. Unlike the last time, Ghua didn't magically show up to help. I carefully scooted forward until the branch started to bow slightly under my weight. The narrower branch made it easier to turn and dangle from my hands. I dropped the three feet to the ground and landed with a soft crunch of dried leaves.

Grabbing the bag, I dug out my knife then took off in the direction of the sounds. Twice, I almost ran into an infected sprinting toward the source of the noise. I moved forward cautiously, using the houses and cars in the streets as cover.

When I found Ghua, I couldn't believe my eyes.

He stood near a woman who lay sobbing uncontrollably on the ground. She was clutching at a dead man beside her. Infected bodies lay in a scattered ring all around them. As I watched, Ghua fought off two more, removing their heads before glancing at the woman.

"You must be quiet," he said. "They will keep coming."

She didn't seem to hear him in her grief. If she didn't stop, she'd bring every infected within miles. She probably already had. We needed to get out of there.

I looked around then sprinted from my cover. Ghua saw me at the same time an infected, hiding behind the opposite house, did. The infected bolted in my direction, its groaning wail echoing down the street. Another answered not far away.

With two infected trailing behind me, I ran all out, the bag bouncing on my back.

Ghua took two steps toward me and motioned for me to run

faster. Behind him, the woman continued to wail. As soon as I passed Ghua, he roared and attacked my two followers. Not pausing, I grabbed the woman by the shoulders and hauled her away from the man. She flopped on the pavement, not even trying to use her legs in her effort to get back to the man.

Tears streamed down her shock-stricken face as her eyes remained locked on the dead man. She needed to snap out of it.

The crack of my hand coming down on her cheek was immediately followed by Ghua's sharp voice.

"Eden!"

However, the slap had done its job. The woman stopped making noise and looked at me with a dazed expression.

"If you want to die, that's fine. But I don't. You need to stop screaming," I said.

Tears continued to stream down her face as she suddenly clutched at me.

"They killed him. They took our kids and killed him when he tried to stop them."

"Who?" I asked.

"The men with guns. They took our kids." She was starting to get loud again.

I grabbed her head between my hands and forced her to look at me instead of the man.

"Do you love them?"

She nodded.

"Then shut up. You can't help them if you're dead."

She sniffled.

"I can't help them, anyway."

Another infected groaned and rushed toward us from around one of the houses. Ghua quickly killed him.

"Come on," I said, releasing her. "We need to get out of

here. You can explain what happened once we're somewhere safer."

"I need my wheelchair."

I jerked back and looked at her again. This time I saw the thinness of her legs through the jeans covering them. I wanted to swear. Instead, I looked around for her wheelchair and found it tipped over nearby and covered with infected blood.

"Ghua, we need that," I said, pointing.

He righted the chair and used his shirt to quickly wipe off the blood.

"Are you hurt anywhere?" I said, focusing on the woman once more.

"No. They left me alone when they had what they wanted. I was useless to them."

Ghua brought the chair over and lifted her into it.

Together, we silently worked our way through the yards to get back to the trees. Ghua killed anything that came at us from between the houses, until the chair got stuck. He scooped up the quiet woman without missing a step.

"Please don't leave my chair," she begged.

Ghua quickly used some wash line from someone's backyard to rig a way for him to carry the chair on his back so he could still use his arms for her.

No one talked as we avoided infected and put more distance between the houses and us.

Just outside of town, we found an old farmhouse. It didn't look like much, but it had heat and water and, after Ghua cleaned it out, no infected.

He carefully set the woman on the couch and looked at her with concern. Her hair, once a cute pixie cut with highlights, had grown out, and now the shaggy mass showed a healthy mix of salt and pepper color. Her bloodshot eyes shifted listlessly around the room.

"I'm Eden," I said, trying to gain her attention. "What's your name?"

"Nancy."

"Nancy, who took your kids?"

"I don't know. We never saw them before. We were in town for a supply run. I was guarding the car. Russ and the kids were working together to clear the houses. I heard their truck before I saw it."

Fresh tears started rolling down her cheeks.

"The men in the back jumped out and pulled me from my chair before I could get a shot off. The kids heard them laughing and came out from the house they were searching. Zachy put an arrow through the hand of one of the men. They threatened me with a knife to get the kids into the back of their truck and to keep Russ away."

"The last thing my kids saw was their dad get shot when he tried to stop them from leaving with our babies."

Her gaze focused on me.

"Will you help me find them?"

"Do you have any idea where they went?"

She shook her head, and hopeless despair clouded her gaze once more.

"They just told my daughter, Brenna, that she'd be safer in their bunker."

My stomach dropped.

"How old is she?"

"Seventeen. Zachy is fifteen."

I looked at Ghua.

"I think it's the same men who took me."

Ghua bared his teeth, which made Nancy gasp. She started crying again in earnest as she gripped my hand. Terror lit in her eyes as she stared at Ghua.

"What is he?"

"Help. A friend," I said.

A low moan sounded from outside.

"Stay here," Ghua said.

He went outside, closing the door firmly behind him. I faced Nancy, squatting down in front of her to hold her attention.

"Did the men say why they took your kids?"

"They said they were running short on help and liked Zachy's skill with the bow."

I wanted to swear. They weren't running short on help. They were running short on women.

"I want to help you, but we'll never be able to get them on our own. There's at least a dozen of those gunmen. The men who took your children will keep them safe from the infected and hellhounds. I promise. Zachy and Brenna will also have enough food to keep them fed through the winter."

She stared at me a moment, shrewdly focused.

"What aren't you telling me?"

I looked down, unable to meet her gaze.

"They believe the human race is dying and want to do their part to keep that from happening."

I watched understanding followed by despair storm into her expression.

"They're going to rape my daughter?" she said.

"I don't know," I answered honestly. "I wasn't raped while I was there. The guy interested in me, Van, kept trying to find other ways to coax me into his bed willingly. Extra portions of food. More shower time. I didn't take anything from him because I didn't want to pay for it."

"But she's only seventeen."

"And I'm barely nineteen. Age doesn't matter to them."

Her gaze shifted to something over my shoulder, and she cringed.

I turned and found Ghua standing just inside the door.

His gaze remained locked on me, and with a sinking feeling in my stomach, I knew why he couldn't seem to look away from me. He'd heard. My time at the kiddy table was over.

Now, I'd learn the truth about his darker intentions. Because I was officially fair game.

Twelve

Our gazes remained locked, and my pulse jumped into overtime. Ghua's indecipherable expression made it hard to know what to do. Just how mad was he? I had no chance of trying to run; he'd proven that. Even the thought of fighting him off was a joke. Was he going to throw me over his shoulder now and take me upstairs?

The image of him naked and swinging free shoved its way forward into my mind, and I glanced to where Dongzilla was thankfully still hidden and undisturbed in his pants. That had to be a good thing, right?

When I looked back up at Ghua, he shifted his gaze to Nancy.

"We will find Brenna and Zachy," he said.

I glanced at the woman and saw the hope blooming in her eyes and hated that I was about to kill it.

"How?" I asked Ghua. "I mean, I know they're in the bunker, but I don't know where that is from here."

"I remember where I found you. I can take us there," he answered without looking at me.

"And then what? We wouldn't stand a chance against the gunmen even if we did find the bunker. They have a lot of guns and are dug in well enough that the hounds and infected can't even get in. You'll die trying, then they'll take Nancy and me, too."

"I don't care," Nancy said. "I just want to be with my kids."

I turned on her.

"Do you hear yourself? You don't care that he'll die or that I'll be raped, just so long as you can be with your kids; and do what for them? Watch them get abused? You've survived this long because you're not stupid. Stop thinking like a mom and think like a survivor. Your kids will not die while they're with Oscar's group. We need more help if you want to have any chance of getting them back."

"Who?" she demanded. "If you haven't noticed, there's a shortage of healthy people around." "Ghua said there are more people where he's from. More people like him."

I looked at Ghua who still stood by the door, wondering if I was telling the truth. Based on our conversations, I'd gotten the impression they had similar appearances and were all looking for females. Would Nancy's daughter's fate be any different with them than Oscar's men?

"Will your people help us?" Nancy asked, looking at Ghua as well.

"Yes."

"Then let's go," she said. "How long will it take to get to them?"

He glanced at the chair he'd set in the middle of the room.

"Three or four days."

"No," she said softly. "A week before we can get my children out of there?" A tremble in her voice made her catch on the last word.

"Don't think like that," I said. "A week won't be too long."

She nodded but looked unconvinced.

"What if we use a car?" she asked. "Could we get there

faster?"

Ghua was quick to say we would.

Nancy met my worried gaze. We both know what troubles a car would bring. The infected could hear well and many were smart enough to lay traps along the road.

I glanced toward the window, reluctantly weighing the odds of survival if I stayed versus if I tried to strike out on my own. Going to the place where the grey men kept their harem had always sounded like a bad idea. Heading there so they could rescue kids from the humans who were trying to breed a brighter future was a sure way to end up on my back for someone. Not a position that interested me. Yet, dead on my own didn't sound so fun either.

Large grey hands settled lightly on my shoulders, and I cringed.

"No, Eden," Ghua said. "You will not run again. Nancy, watch Eden while I check the garage for a car. Yell if she tries to leave."

* * * *

It felt so unbelievably normal to be behind the wheel again, despite the static only radio stations, the cars randomly stopped on the roads, and the infected who insisted on running out in front of me. I used my wipers to try to clean the blood-smeared windshield.

"You'd think it would be gas that you run out of first," Nancy said from the passenger seat. "But it's the washer fluid. We usually kept two extra gallons in the back."

Instead of two jugs of fluid in the back of the truck, I had one Ghua. He still hadn't said anything about my lie, and he'd had plenty of time. Not alone time, though. I glanced at Nancy, grateful for her presence even though I resented her for her unwillingness to quietly let me try to run.

If you run, he'll waste time looking for you instead of getting the help my kids need.

Her words echoed in my head as I swerved around another car.

Ghua thumped on the roof of the truck. It wasn't because of my driving. He had amazingly sharp eyesight and had probably seen something in the road ahead that I hadn't yet. I slowed to a stop and rolled down my window enough to hear him.

"The sun is setting. We need to get off this road and find a place to stay for the night," he said.

I started up again and took the next road to the right, which got us off the highway. I followed it for several miles before taking a left onto a dirt drive. The narrow lane felt like it went on forever, and when the ruts deepened, I thought it would dead end at a field. Finally, I spotted a small farmhouse around the next bend.

"We'll be lucky if the roof doesn't leak," Nancy said, leaning forward to peer at it. "There's no way it will have lights."

I parked by the house and killed the engine, quietly sharing her sentiment. Hints of white paint showed on the grey-weathered, wood siding. One of the porch supports had collapsed and parts of the floor were missing.

"I'll tell him that we—"

The truck bounced as Ghua jumped out of the back.

I quickly rolled down my window.

"I don't think there's going to be electricity here."

He grunted and kept walking. It was pretty much the same reaction he'd been giving since we left the other place almost an hour ago.

We watched him inspect the front door then walk around the side of the house.

"What is he?" Nancy asked quietly.

"I don't know. I was on my own a few days ago when he just showed up, killed all the infected around me, and told me he would protect me."

"Wow. That sounds nice."

"Yeah, he also pretty much told me that he planned to have sex with me once I was eighteen."

She looked at me.

"But you said you were nineteen."

"Yeah. Well, I told him I was twelve."

Her mouth dropped open a little.

"Oh."

"Yeah. Oh."

"Still want to run?" she asked.

"Not tonight. I'd never get far on foot, and he'd hear this thing leave."

A light went on inside the house, illuminating the window right in front of the truck.

"What are you going to do?" Nancy asked.

"I don't know." I wanted to tell myself that he'd been reasonable so far, but in reality, he hadn't been. He hadn't let me leave. He'd said it was because I was a kid and couldn't take care of myself, but even after he knew my age, he'd told Nancy to yell if I tried. So, what did that tell me? He still had a plan for me.

"You were right," Nancy said. "It's not fair that I put you in harm's way for my kids. But, I'd do the same thing again. I'm sorry."

"I get it. It's the world we've always lived in. Each person for themselves."

Ghua rounded the corner of the house and went straight for Nancy's door.

"We'll stay here tonight," he said, only looking at her. He held out his hand toward me, though.

"I'll take the keys."

I handed them over and got out to grab our things from the back. The weight of the bag on my shoulder gave me a sense of security because of the knife inside. I wouldn't be defenseless.

With the mop weapon in hand, I closed the door and followed the pair around the house. A whisper of noise behind me was all the warning I had before something pulled on the bag. Letting it slide off my shoulder, I gripped the mop and turned.

The old farmer's barely clouded eyes tracked my move. As I jabbed forward, aiming for his throat, he dropped the bag and lifted his hand. The jagged metal end went through his palm with ease. He slowly extended his arm to the side, moving my only weapon out of the way.

His gaze shifted to the right at the sound of a low growl behind me.

Ghua rushed past me and gripped the man's head between both his hands.

"Look away, Eden."

I turned my head just in time to avoid the spray of blood.

Nancy was nowhere behind us. Before I could wonder what Ghua had done with her, something thumped on the ground; and Ghua gripped my shoulders.

He jerked me toward him, his fierce gaze sweeping over my face.

"Did it bite you?"

I shook my head as I noted the blood that dotted his cheek

and forehead.

"Why didn't you call for help?"

He shook me ever so slightly.

"You were right there."

"No, I was not. I asked you to open the door, and you weren't behind me."

"Are you seriously scolding me because you weren't paying attention?"

He growled in my face. It wasn't the same sound as what he'd done just before removing Old McDonald's head. This growl sounded like something I would do if I had a can of food but no can opener.

"Go inside, Eden." Each word was clipped.

I left the bag and rushed toward the house.

Nancy was pulling herself up into one of the kitchen chairs around the table.

"What happened?" she asked, catching sight of me. "You're covered in blood."

"An infected found me."

"Were you bitten?" Suspicion and fear crept into her gaze.

"No. No bites."

"Then go clean up. You don't want that stuff on you longer than necessary."

I nodded, grabbed a knife from the counter just to be safe, and went further into the house. The place looked much better on the inside than it had on the outside. Not clean exactly, just not as run down. Everything looked original from the 1940's, though.

The bathroom had a sink with two separate taps for hot and cold. I started both and looked at myself in the mirror. Blood was starting to dry on the side of my neck and in my hair. I grabbed the hand towel and wetted it to start wiping the gore away. My effort made a worse mess the further back I worked. I stopped and turned slightly. The back of my jacket was covered with gore, too. That would only mean my hair was the same.

I turned off the water and started to strip. Nancy was right. I didn't want the infected's blood on me any longer than necessary.

A shower arm with a circular curtain rod extended over a claw foot tub. I pulled back the curtain and turned on the taps. It took a minute for the water to warm. I didn't wait. I stepped into the cold spray, turning my back to it. I gasped at the temperature but didn't step out of the water. Tipping my head up, I let it rinse away the dark blood. When I thought I'd rinsed it all clean, I soaped up everything. By then, the water had warmed and steam began to fill the space inside the curtain.

A whisper of noise outside the curtain made me freeze. I fisted my right hand, wishing I hadn't been stupid enough to leave the knife resting on the sink's ledge. I still had a chance, though. A forearm against the throat would keep infected teeth away so I could call for help.

Gritting my teeth, I gripped the curtain and ripped it open.

Ghua looked up from the clean clothes he'd been setting on the closed toilet lid. For a stunned moment, we both just stared at each other. Then, his gaze dipped, taking in the fully nude front view I'd just given him. The dirty clothes that he'd held in his other arm fell to the floor.

I squeaked and ripped the curtain shut. My heart pounded in my chest, and I struggled not to cry as I stared at the curtain, waiting for him to open it again. I'd fight him; I wouldn't give in. But I knew, in the end, he would win.

"I know why you lied," he said softly.

I shivered despite the hot water still pounding my skin.

"I heard what you said about the human men who wanted you for sex. You think I'm the same. So you fear me. You fear the infected. You fear dying. You are so full of fear, you're afraid of living too, Eden."

The door clicked shut.

I peeked around the curtain and found myself alone in the bathroom. A clean, large t-shirt waited on the toilet along with a pair of men's once white briefs. I shut off the water and dried off with a towel I found in a slim open-shelved cabinet at the end of the tub.

Ghua was wrong. I wasn't afraid to live. That's all I wanted to do. But everything around me was determined to make my crappy life as hard and scary as possible.

I tugged the shirt over my head and held up the underwear. The dingy grey that was once white didn't bother me. Even the darker stripe on the back didn't bother me as much as it would have months ago. However, there was no way I could wear them. The old farmer had been a big man. The underwear would never stay up around my waist. Two of me could fit in them. I put them on the shelves by the towels.

The shirt was long enough to keep me decent until I could search through the farmer's clothes myself.

I opened the door and almost screamed at the sight of Ghua, who waited in the hall. He was missing his shirt but still had his blood-spattered pants on.

"Nancy needs to use the bathroom," he said. "I need to shower first."

I nodded and hurried past him down the hall. From the kitchen, I could hear the water turn on and knew he'd left the door open.

"Looks like you got it all," Nancy said. She lifted a can. "Is this what he's been feeding you?"

"If you don't want it, I'll eat yours."

I grabbed the second can and spoon that waited on the table and started eating.

Nancy made a face, and I turned to look through the cabinets. There wasn't a whole lot. A few spices, a can of creamed corn, and a stick of butter that stank. I checked the fridge and quickly slammed it shut.

"It's creamed corn or the dog food. I'd go with the dog food. More calories and you won't stay awake listening to the hellhounds because your stomach is trying to eat itself."

She sighed and lifted a spoonful to her mouth.

"Needs salt," she said after she swallowed her first bite. I found the salt shaker and passed it to her.

"I'm going to check upstairs."

Upstairs consisted of three small bedrooms. One was full of forgotten pieces of furniture, boxes, and a ton of papers.

The farmer's bedroom was easily identifiable by the lingering hint of manure smell and the unmade bed. The sheets looked like they hadn't been changed in ages. Ignoring the bed, I started digging through his dresser. Ghua had honestly brought me the best there'd been to offer. At the bottom of the last drawer, I found a clean set of embroidered sheets neatly wrapped in tissue paper.

They'd obviously been put away as a keepsake. But, the person to whom they would have been important was long gone. Shaking them out, I remade the bed. By the time I finished, Ghua walked past the room with Nancy in his arms.

I hurried after him.

"I remade the bed in here. Nancy and I can share."

Ignoring me, he set Nancy on the single bed in the adjoining room.

"If you need something, call for me," he told her.

She nodded, her gaze darting to me before she rolled to her side toward the wall.

I couldn't exactly be mad at her. She didn't want to risk pissing off the person willing to help her save her kids.

I turned and went back to the only other room. My heart felt heavy and cold as I stared at the bed from the doorway. I couldn't bring myself to walk any closer. I liked Ghua, but I didn't want to do this. I didn't want to be left behind and die, either.

Slowly, I moved toward the bed and crawled under the covers. It took several minutes before the bed dipped behind me. Ghua's arms snaked around my waist, and he pulled me tight against his chest.

I trembled and tried not to think. May told me once that she thought of other things. It made what Oscar's men did to her pass more quickly.

Ghua's exhale tickled my ear, and his hand stroked down my arm.

"Sleep, Eden. You can be twelve for as long as you want."

The tears I'd been struggling to hold back began to fall.

Thirteen

As sobs shook my shoulders, Ghua held me close and continued to stroke my hair. He also started talking.

"I have only been on the surface a short time, but I have learned much. Not just about the beauty up here but about my past, too. A past I don't remember.

"My brothers and I once belonged to a race tied to the land. We had pale skin, lighter than yours, and loved the sun as much as you do. We had homes and families, and we were happy. But, my people had to leave. The trees, our life source and connection to the land, were dying. We set out in groups, all in search of a new life source. In a new land, my brothers and I found the crystals in caverns below the surface.

"The crystals fed our power to nurture the plants and trees. We helped things grow and flourish in those caverns. However, not all of our people agreed that the energy of the crystals was natural. Divided because of fear, my people trapped my brothers and me underground where we have lived a never-ending life.

"It wasn't until Mya touched the source crystal that we discovered all of this and the reason for the hellhounds. Our people placed a curse on us and the creatures with us. The hellhounds are here because of our past actions. Mya helped us understand it's our responsibility to aid the humans who have survived.

"That is all I am doing, Eden. I am helping you survive. I swear I will not hurt you. Please, do not cry. Each tear is leaving a scar on my heart."

Whether I wanted to admit it or not, I'd been standing on the edge of trusting Ghua for a while. And, his pleading tone and soft words made it impossible not to fall. Everything he'd said before he knew my age, I'd dismissed as a lie. But now, I knew better. He hadn't lied. Not once. Ghua was different in so many ways from us humans. Including, it seemed, his capacity for kindness.

As I embraced that fragile feeling of trust, I struggled against the ache in my chest and realized that I wasn't alone anymore. I didn't have to keep running. I didn't need to fight against everything by myself. The relief that came with those realizations only made me shake more.

I turned in his arms and met his gaze. He reached up and wiped my tears away, his eyes reflecting the sorrow and misery I'd felt moments ago.

"I'm sorry I kept trying to run," I said.

"Do not apologize. You did nothing wrong. I never should have told you that I hoped you would consider me as something more than what I am."

I frowned.

"I don't know what you mean. What are you?"

"A stranger in your world."

I studied his yellow-green eyes for a long moment. They no longer seemed so foreign. His proud brow and stubborn chin looked just as human as any other man's. In that moment, I realized I'd stopped seeing the color of his skin, too. He was just Ghua, the man who continued to be so patient with me.

"You're not strange anymore. At least, not to me. How did

you want me to see you?"

"As a man you might someday love."

That wasn't at all what I'd gotten out of anything he'd said to me before now.

"So you're not taking me back to your home so that you or someone else can rape me?"

He growled low.

"No one will touch your pussy without your permission."

I choked a little, hearing him say it so bluntly, and looked down at his bare chest for a moment.

"Not even you?" I asked.

"Not even me, Eden." His thumb gently stroked over my cheek. "But thank you for letting me see it in the bathroom. It is very pretty."

With those words, I realized how ridiculously naïve Ghua was, and how grossly I'd misunderstood him and his intentions in so many ways.

Looking up, I lightly kissed his cheek.

"Thank you for keeping me safe. Even from myself."

He grunted.

"Go to sleep, Eden."

I closed my eyes and let myself relax.

* * * *

Sweat coated my skin, and I kicked off the stifling hot blankets. Cool air swept over my legs, and my sigh of relief changed to a jaw-cracking yawn.

The fingers stroking my stomach stilled, and Ghua moved beside me, his weight shifting from the mattress like he was sitting up. I blinked at the light filling the room and stretched languidly while my eyes focused.

Ghua made a pained sound, and I heard him inhale deeply.

The mattress between my legs dipped, and several things clicked into place at once. My shirt had ridden up to my bellybutton. I had no underwear on. Kicking off the covers had left me exposed to Ghua's very focused and very curious gaze.

He was leaned over me, studying my lady bits from only inches away.

I made a panicked sound and scrambled off the bed so the shirt fell back into place. It didn't seem to matter. His eyes remained fixed on the apex of my legs as if he could see right through the material.

"You said you wouldn't touch me," I said, my voice shaking.

He looked up at me.

"I didn't. I wanted to, but I didn't. I only looked. I've wanted to see a real pussy for a long time. Yours is so pretty."

His words were so emphatically sincere I didn't know what to think. A flush crept into my cheeks as he continued to meet my gaze.

"Well, you shouldn't look at me like you did, either."

"I'm sorry, Eden. I didn't know. Is it okay to smell your pussy? It smells so good."

"No. No smelling either."

His shoulders sagged as he nodded, and I almost grinned at the sheer disappointment on his face.

"Nancy is awake. I will help her downstairs," he said, standing.

The massive erection tenting the front of his pants made my mouth pop open. If I'd thought him huge before, I didn't know how to classify him now.

He noticed the direction of my gaze.

"You can look at me," he said, reaching for his waistband. "I don't mind."

"No, no!" I said quickly, waving my hands and averting my eyes. "That's okay. It wouldn't be appropriate for me to look."

"Why not?"

I scrambled to think of a reason he would believe.

"Because Nancy's awake and looking at each other is the kind of thing that couples do—"

His face instantly lit with hope, and I quickly started over to clarify we weren't a couple.

"I mean it's something that only couples should do together. And only when they are alone. It's private."

"Oh. Okay."

He gave me one last look filled with so much yearning my heart started to beat faster. Then, he left the room to help Nancy downstairs.

I collapsed on the bed and struggled to let my mind catch up with what had just happened. Ghua had seen under my hood. He could have tried to force things. But he hadn't. Instead, I'd told him no, and he'd walked away. And, not angrily. Just a little disappointed. Okay, maybe a lot disappointed.

A slow smile spread on my face. He'd kept his word. All of it. Why did that make me want to run after him and hug him?

My smile withered just as quickly as it had appeared when I realized how underdressed I still was.

I left the room and jogged downstairs, hoping to find out what he'd done with my clothes from yesterday. Although some of them were covered in infected blood, I'd need to use what I could. I didn't want to go walking around in just a t-shirt, no matter how awesome it felt.

However, when I reached the first floor, I couldn't find Ghua. The kitchen was empty, and when I knocked on the bathroom door, Nancy said she was in there by herself.

"Where'd he go?" I asked.

"Dunno. He asked if I needed help. I said I didn't, and he closed the door. Now, if you don't mind, I'd like a few minutes to myself."

The words didn't offend me. Most of what she'd said had sounded strained like I'd interrupted her crying.

"If you need help, let me know," I said.

"Thanks."

I left her and checked the rest of the lower level. Passing the living room window, I caught sight of Ghua standing in front of the truck. Something dark was smeared across the hood, ending next to a chunk of metal. Ghua circled around the truck, looked in the bed, then scanned the rest of the yard. I did the same.

Nancy's wheelchair slowly rolled out of the barn's gaping door. Ghua took a step in that direction, and I pounded on the window.

When he looked back at me, I shook my head.

"It's a trap," I said to myself, knowing he couldn't hear. "Don't go in there. Come back inside by us."

His lips parted, and he smiled at me sweetly.

"I will be fine, my Eden," he called.

While he still looked at me, the door behind him swung open. A herd of infected swarmed out of the barn, running at Ghua, who was waving farewell at me. My heart stuttered.

Not him. Not now.

"No!" I yelled. "Behind you!"

I slapped my hand against the window and stared in horror as the first infected reached him. She bit into his exposed shoulder.

Ghua's smile changed to a roar. He reached back and ripped

her head off. And that was the last thing I saw before Ghua was lost under an avalanche of infected.

Spinning away from the window, I raced to the kitchen. I needed to get out there to help him. My eyes swept over the knives on the counter before I stopped myself. What had I told Nancy? Stop thinking like a mom, and think like a survivor. I needed to think. What would happen if I ran out there now? I had no weapon. No protective layers to deflect a bite.

Swearing, I turned back toward the living room and stopped at the sight of Nancy dragging herself down the hall.

"What's happening?" she asked.

"Ghua's outside," I said. "There's infected all over in the yard."

She paled.

"Get me a knife."

She was right. The infected would try to get in the house, next. I grabbed us both a weapon, quickly gave her one, then went back to the window.

Ghua, please be dead so I don't have to kill you, I thought to myself.

However, the sight outside the window stopped all thought while I stood there in shock.

"What do you see?" Nancy asked after several moments of my silence.

"Bodies. A lot of headless bodies." There had to be at least twenty of them. They spilled over the barren yard like a bunch of toppled dolls. I scanned each one for a hint of grey skin.

"I don't see Ghua." My heart ached with what that might mean.

"Are they still fighting?" she asked.

"No. There aren't any infected moving out there."

We both heard the door in the kitchen open. Nancy and I shared a look. She pulled her legs under her and leaned back against a chair, her knife up and ready. We both watched the doorway and listened to the steps that rasped across the kitchen floor.

Covered head to toe in blood, Ghua stepped into the opening. His eyes met mine. They weren't cloudy. Yet. Bites covered his arms and shoulders. There were even a few on his ribs.

Nancy swore.

"We need to get to the truck before he turns," she said.

Ghua's gaze shifted to her.

"Infected bites don't make me sick. And, the truck will do you no good. They removed pieces of it. But, your chair still rolls well."

Hope flooded me at the first words he'd spoken.

"Are you sure you can't get sick?" I asked.

"Everyone gets sick," Nancy said harshly. "If the truck doesn't work, we're fucked." She tossed her knife aside as tears started rolling down her cheeks.

I ignored her and continued to wait for Ghua's answer.

His gaze met mine and softened.

"I will not become stupid and want to bite you. I will not hurt you, Eden. Ever."

He hadn't lied to me yet. And, I didn't see why he would start now.

With a shout of relief, I ran to him, but he stopped me with a raised hand.

"No, Eden. I cannot touch you like this."

I nodded and stepped back.

"All the infected are dead. I checked around the barn too,

to be sure. We're safe for now but should leave soon. I will wash this off. The door will stay open. Call me if you see something."

I cringed as he turned to leave. Bites covered his back as well. I remembered what he'd told me about getting shot. That it hurt. And, I bet all those bites hurt a lot, too.

While he started the shower, I ran upstairs to get our bag and brought it to the bathroom. His bloody pants lay on the floor, and the curtain was already closed around him.

"I brought the bag with your clothes."

"Thank you."

Pink slashed the yellowed curtain as he washed.

"Are the bites still bleeding?" I asked.

"Yes. It will take a while for them to heal."

I opened the old mirror cabinet above the sink and grabbed the pain relievers and bandages. There were plenty of the former and not enough of the latter.

The water turned off, and I quickly grabbed a towel to thrust in his direction as the curtain slid open.

"Put that around your waist," I said, keeping my gaze averted until he was covered.

Using another towel, I gently began dabbing the bites. The ones that had already stopped bleeding got a bit of peroxide and some ointment. The ones that still bled I put some pressure on until they stopped. The bites on his back were the deepest, and I cringed as I used the bandages on those. When I finished, I moved in front of him and looked at his neck.

Without me asking, he sat on the toilet seat so I could see better. Standing between his legs, I gently cleaned each of the bites ringing his throat as well.

"I like when you touch me," Ghua said.

I looked up and met his steady gaze.

"Okay, but how about next time you just ask me to touch you instead of nearly dying." Although I meant it as a joke, it came out a bit naggy. So, I gentled my tone. "You scared me, Ghua. Don't ever do that again."

"I am sorry, my Eden."

He reached up and smoothed back my errant hair.

"I did not mean to scare you, only to keep you safe."

My heart ached at his words and what I was feeling. He'd been right. My fear had clouded my thinking for so long. It wasn't completely gone, but Ghua's presence was helping me think and see more clearly.

Almost losing him had scared the hell out of me. And, it had also made me realize something very important. I liked him. A lot.

The idea of caring about anyone worried me. I'd be vulnerable and more likely to make stupid mistakes. Like Nancy wanting to charge after her kids without more help. That's what caring did. That's what...love did. That's what I'd been considering doing when I'd grabbed the knives. I felt a jolt of surprise at the direction of my thoughts. Did I really like him that much?

We continued to look at each other as I sorted through the jumble of my thoughts and came to a conclusion. I needed to know just how far my like for Ghua extended. I needed to know if what I felt was just gratitude for keeping me alive or if it was something more.

My gaze dipped to his lips, and my stomach gave a flutter of excitement. An alarming reaction.

Not stopping to consider the consequences, I leaned in to press my lips to his. A tingle of warmth spread through me and intensified as he groaned then growled.

Ghua's hands lifted to cup the back of my head. His mouth brushed lightly over mine a moment before his tongue swept across my lips. I gasped and gripped his arms. He made another low sound and repeated the teasing lick.

Heart pounding, I let him in. The first touch of his tongue to mine fanned the flames spreading within me and made my knees weak. I slid my hands up to his shoulders for support. He growled again and pulled me into his lap without breaking contact.

His heat surrounded me. His fingers trailed down my arm then back up to touch my jaw.

His gentle exploration made me forget that the kiss was supposed to be a test. Lost in the feel and taste of him, I let him take over. His tongue brushed against mine again and again as his hand continued to move restlessly, smoothing over my shoulder and down my arm once more. His fingers laced mine, and he brought my hand to his cheek, showing just how much he wanted me to continue touching him.

I explored the hard planes of his jaw, sinking deeper into the kiss. Needing more of him.

His hands slid down my arms and his fingers brushed my ribs. My breast ached with that simple caress.

I pulled away, gasping for air and shaking with the need for more.

He placed tiny kisses on the corner of my mouth and down my throat. But he didn't go any further. He didn't touch me where my heart thundered under my breast.

He pulled away to look at me, and I stared up, seeing the pale skin of my hand against his dark face. It didn't look weird.

I feathered my trembling fingers over his brow and down his

strong, familiar nose.

"Does this mean you will someday be able to love me?" he asked me softly.

Someday? I feared I didn't have that long to wait.

"Maybe."

He smiled widely, showing all his pointed teeth.

I couldn't grin at all. With that one kiss, I already knew the answer.

Fourteen

I stood and tried to ignore the way his hands dragged over my arms as he reluctantly released me.

"I need my clothes," I said, my throat feeling a bit tight. "The ones you took yesterday."

He sighed.

"The coat is full of infected blood. I threw it out. The rest is on the kitchen chair by the door."

"Thank you." I started to leave the room.

"Eden?"

"Yeah?"

I looked back and found him standing.

"I'm glad you decided you didn't want to be twelve anymore."

"Me too," I said, even though I wasn't. Being twelve around him had been easier.

Finding the clothes at the table just like he'd said, I slipped my underwear back on with a grimace and looked at the pants. There were a few stray dark spots that could be dirt or infected blood. I put them on and hoped for the best. The shirt I left on the chair. The farmer's old shirt worked well enough. Since I wouldn't have a jacket, I started back upstairs, intending to search the closet, but stopped when I passed Nancy sitting in the same spot.

"He hasn't turned, and I don't think he will. If you want your kids saved, stop crying and get ready to leave."

"You sound like a heartless bitch, sometimes," she said as she pushed herself up straighter.

"I am what I need to be. You're here and still alive. I think that means you've been a heartless bitch a few times, too."

Her puffy-lidded gaze swept over me.

"More times than I would like to admit," she said. "He's really okay? How is that possible?"

I shrugged. "He's not human. He's a lot stronger and faster. And, he's lived a very long time. The hellhounds came from where he used to live. Since the hellhounds are the cause of the infected, it makes sense that Ghua would be immune to whatever sickness the infected have."

With athletic shorts hanging low on his hips, Ghua emerged from the hallway. The sight would have been drool worthy if not for all the bite marks covering his exposed skin. Who was I kidding? I still wanted to drool.

"I saw a truck in the barn," he said. "I'm going to check if it works then come back for both of you."

He held out the bag to me, but I hesitated to take it.

"Don't you want a shirt?"

"Not until the bites dry."

I grabbed the bag, and he used it to reel me closer. His hand cupped the back of my head, and he set his forehead to mine. The way he lightly brushed his nose against mine set my heart racing again.

He grinned, showing that he could hear it, and left me after one last nuzzle. The door banged shut behind him.

"Are you okay?" Nancy asked softly. "Did he hurt you last night?"

I turned to look at her, seeing real worry on her face.

"I'm okay. He actually is as kind as he says. He didn't do anything."

Her eyes started to water again, and she quickly looked away.

"I hope the men who have my kids are the same."

"Me too."

I left before she could question the hint of doubt that had been in my voice.

Unsure how many more times I would need clean clothes, I raided everything I could use from the farmer's room. He had three threadbare button-up flannel shirts that I layered over the t-shirt I now wore. He also had an old, wool military jacket. I put that on, too, knowing I'd need the warmth.

By the time I walked down the stairs, Ghua and Nancy sat at the kitchen table with a road atlas open in front of her.

"What are you guys doing?" I asked.

"Trying to determine where we are so we can figure out how to get to where we're going. I was in Atoka, Oklahoma when you found me," Nancy said, pointing at the town on the map.

"What is the name of the place you said your people are at?" I asked Ghua.

"My people are staying in Tolerance, near Whiteman. Tolerance is a subdivision. Whiteman, a military base."

"In what state?"

He shrugged.

"How long will it take for us to get there?" Nancy asked.

"In the truck? We might reach Tolerance by nightfall if we do not run into any more infected traps."

"The truck worked, then?"

He nodded and took a shirt from the bag I set on the table. I watched him carefully tug it over his head and hoped, for all our sakes, we got to Tolerance without incident.

"I'm pretty sure it's north," I said as Nancy continued to study the map. "North was the direction Ghua was headed before I turned us east."

"Yes," Ghua agreed. "It's almost straight north of here."

"That helps."

Ghua stood and scooped up Nancy from her chair.

"You can look at your picture in the truck."

She didn't argue, but I caught the resentful glare she shot Ghua. The surge of annoyance rose inside of me. Nancy might not be done looking at the map, but he was right; we needed to get going. Daylight didn't last forever. Yet, I knew that wasn't the full reason behind my attitude. Ghua was nice, and I wanted to defend him. Dangerous territory.

After a moment of hesitation, I grabbed our bag and reached the door in time to watch Ghua gently place Nancy on the bench seat.

Ghua turned and saw me.

"Are you ready?" he asked.

Ready to leave? Yes. Ready to find better clothes? Yes. Ready to eat something other than dog food? Always. But, was I ready to go to his home where hundreds more of his kind lived? No. That worried the hell out of me because, once I was there, would I ever leave?

He tilted his head then closed the door to come to me.

"What is it?" he asked.

"You were right. I'm afraid of everything."

He smiled and pressed his forehead to mine.

"I will keep you safe."

"Not from everything," I said, thinking of my heart.

"I swear," he said with complete sincerity, utterly clueless of the damage those words caused.

I eased away from him.

"We better get going. Daylight's limited."

He grunted and walked with me to the driver's seat. Once I was in, he jumped in the back where he already had Nancy's chair loaded.

* * * *

We pulled up before a massive barrier that rose at least fifteen feet high. It looked like it was made out of everything from sinks to metal pallets to full sized cars planted into the ground on their tail ends. As I turned off the engine, the headlights of the vehicle in front of us came on. The beams shot straight up into the pre-dusk sky. Forty feet away, another vehicle's lights came on and down the wall the lights went, illuminating one by one.

The truck bounced as Ghua jumped from the bed. Dried infected blood clung to his face, hair, and bare chest. He'd tossed his shirt after only an hour. The infected hadn't made getting here easy. He'd killed more of them than I could count. Not that it made a dent in how many were still out there.

"Stay in the truck," he said through the window glass. I hadn't rolled it down since he'd warned me not to open it or get out, after our first stop.

"Why? What are you doing?"

He glanced at Nancy before meeting my gaze.

"Getting help. I can't carry either of you like this."

"Okay. Just hurry up."

He nodded, and I watched in amazement as he climbed up and over the wall with ease.

"Shit," Nancy said beside me. "Even if my legs worked, I'm not sure I could free climb a vertical wall like that."

"He sure does make it look easy."

Both Nancy and I jumped a moment later when several grey men dropped from the wall in front of us.

Ghua dropped down last and walked our way. He spoke softly to the other men. One went around to the back of the truck and got Nancy's chair. Another went around to Nancy's side of the truck and opened the door.

"May I carry you inside?" he asked.

"Sure." The word came out as a dry rasp, and I knew she was freaking out.

I'd be a liar if I didn't admit to doing the same thing. They were all like Ghua. Reptilian eyes, pointed ears, very sharp teeth, and an issue with wearing shirts. That didn't worry me as much as the fact that I didn't know them. My trust only extended to Ghua.

The man scooped her up into his arms, watching her closely.

"I am Kerr," he said.

"My name's Nancy."

"I will not drop you, Nancy."

"Thanks."

My door opened. I turned, expecting Ghua. Instead, it was some other guy. My heart started to hammer as he reached for me, skipping the polite request to pick me up. He lifted me out of the truck and started toward the wall, his gaze skimming over my face.

A tiny voice started to whisper in my mind. This was where it would all change. All the promises of not forcing things would go out the window, and I'd be passed around like everyone's new favorite toy. Thoughts of everything May had endured swamped me, and I struggled to keep my shit together.

"Stop," Ghua said.

The man carrying me halted and turned toward Ghua, who was only a step behind us.

"Put her down, Uan."

The man holding me gently set me on my feet. Ghua moved close, his gaze searching mine.

"You're afraid. Why?"

"I don't know what you're talking about."

He tilted his head.

"Your heart is racing."

"So?"

He grunted and looked up at the wall where Nancy had already disappeared. After a moment, he met my gaze.

"Would you like to be twelve again, Eden?"

My chest started to ache. He knew. He understood. I blinked, struggling not to give in to my tears.

"Yes."

He looked at Uan.

"Eden is twelve. A child. She cannot have sex with anyone until she says she's old enough."

Uan looked at me.

"I understand. May I carry you inside?"

I nodded. A moment later, I was up in his arms and over the wall. The speed in which Uan moved made me a bit sick. But I was on my feet, in a grassy clearing just on the outskirts of a large subdivision, before I could fully feel the effects. Ghua stood beside me, watching me closely. He wasn't the only one.

Men were gathered around, most of them staring at Nancy in Kerr's arms.

"You do not walk?" one asked.

"No," she said. "I can't. My legs don't work."

"Why?" another asked.

"Because I was in an accident several years ago."

"All right," a female voice called from the back. "Break it up. Let me through." The men parted, and a young woman around my age strode forward.

"Hi, I'm Mya," she said, looking at Nancy and me. "Sorry if the questions are intrusive. These guys are still learning about our world and the rules."

"It's all right," Nancy said. "Do you think I could sit in my chair?"

"Will you be able to move it on the grass or would it be easier on the street?"

Nancy looked up at the guy holding her.

"I promise you're fine," Mya said. "They like helping."

"But only females, right?" I couldn't help but ask.

Mya grinned slightly as she looked at me.

"They're a lot friendlier to us, that's for sure. Can I ask what your names are?"

Ghua spoke up before I could.

"This is Eden. She is twelve."

Mya's brows shot up, and she studied me for a moment.

"Is she the one?" she asked, her attention shifting to Ghua.

"Yes," he said.

Surprise lit Mya's face. Before I could ask why, Nancy spoke up from Kerr's arms.

"I'm Nancy. And I need your help." She started to cry, drawing everyone's attention.

Mya moved closer to Nancy.

"What happened?" Mya said.

"My husband was killed, and my children were taken from

me. I have to get them back. Please. I need help."

A chorus of, "I will help Nancy," rang out around us.

"Hold on," Mya said, waving for them to be quiet. She focused on Nancy.

"We'll help any way we can. Do you know where your children are? Who took them, and why?"

"Eden knows where they are. I think they took my kids to be workers and," Nancy started sniffling louder. "And, I think they're going to force my daughter." She turned, covered her face with her hands, and had a good cry. I couldn't blame her.

"Force her daughter to do what?" one of the men behind her asked.

Mya ignored the question as she faced the men around her.

"This is something we need to discuss with Molev," she said. "Finish lighting up the wall and meet at my house."

She looked at Nancy, who was wiping her face.

"Nancy, if it's okay with you, Kerr will run you to my house. You can use one of my guest rooms on the first floor. Uan, can you follow with her chair. I'll be right behind you."

Nancy made some kind of response that Kerr must have taken as a yes because he took off running. Many of the others followed. Some ran along the walls, and more lights shot up into the increasing dusk.

"They won't last forever," I said, looking at the batteries set on the ground and wired to the lights.

"They don't need to," Mya said. "They only need to last until the hounds are dead."

I made a sound of disbelief.

"The hounds don't die."

She smiled slightly.

"There's a lot you don't know, Eden. A lot I don't know,

either, like why Ghua thinks you're twelve."

"She's afraid we will have sex with her," Ghua said, speaking up. "The men who tried taking her, the same ones who have Nancy's children, wanted sex. They made Eden hungry and used food to try to persuade her. She feels safer with us when she says she's twelve."

My mouth popped open, and I stared at Ghua.

"The fey are a lot smarter than they let on," Mya said.

"Fey?"

Ghua continued to watch me with the same expression that I'd once taken as a curious, open study because he was clueless about me. I now knew better.

"He didn't tell you their history?" Mya asked.

"He did. A bit. His people were divided in their beliefs about some crystal, and he and his brothers were trapped under the earth." I also recalled how he'd said he'd once been paler than me.

"His people were the fey from our legends, with powers and everything. They made things grow. They weren't bad but made some bad decisions. The rest of their people died while these guys continued to live, trapped in their caves. These guys aren't bad, but they are paying for the consequences of the decisions their people made a very long time ago."

It'd been obvious from his appearance that he wasn't human. But fey? My mind grappled with that idea for a moment before the rest of what she said sunk in.

"Why are you telling me this?" I asked.

"Because they deserve a chance to be treated fairly."

"Don't we all?"

She nodded for me to start walking with her.

"Why did you seem surprised that Ghua likes me?"

She frowned at me in confusion.

"You asked if I was the one, and when he said yes, you seemed surprised."

"Oh. I didn't mean if he liked you. He's been looking for you, specifically, for a while now."

"What?"

"I don't know what it's really like out there," Mya said. "I've been lucky. When the first wave of earthquakes and hellhounds came, Drav found me before anything could happen. He's kept me safe and fairly sheltered from it all. I can't imagine what it's been like for you."

"It's been shit."

"I bet," she said sympathetically. "When the bombs started, Drav took me to their underground city. Ghua was sent back up here to round up the other fey until the bombing stopped."

I remembered the bombing and how the first group of raiders had insisted we keep scavenging the smaller towns because they had feared the bombings would start up again and destroy everything.

"While Ghua was here, he saw a girl and her family. Turns out that girl was you. At the time, you were with too many other people with guns for him to talk to you. So he listened, learned more of our language, and discovered that you needed food. He collected what he could in a house cleared of infected and led you to it. He told me that he had wanted you safe from the bombs before he had to return to Ernisi. If he would have had any idea that the people you were with were using you, he wouldn't have left you. He didn't even tell us about seeing other people until recently, when he left to go find you again."

I tried to wrap my head around the idea that Ghua hadn't just stumbled upon me a few days ago and taken a liking to me.

"Tell us who took the children," Molev said, looking at me.

"Men," I said with a shrug, unsure what he was expecting.

"What Molev means is, what can you tell us about the men who took them?"

"Well, there are about twelve gunmen." I frowned. "Maybe less now. Ghua may have killed one of the men who tried to take me back."

"I did not kill him, Mya," Ghua said as he came up behind me and placed his hands on my shoulders.

I exhaled and leaned into his touch a little, feeling calmer and grateful that cleaning up hadn't taken him very long.

"There were eight of us workers before I left. Nine, now, with Nancy's kids," I said with a glance at her. "They are holed up in an underground bunker. There's only one way in, through a steel reinforced door that can lock from the inside. They have a lot of guns and a lot of ammunition and plenty of supplies to last the winter if they chose not to open that door again until spring."

"What are the workers for?" Mya asked.

"Mostly to search the field for forgotten vegetables. Withered, soft, it didn't matter. Fresh food meant not touching the supplies."

"You said mostly. What about when they aren't searching for food?" she asked.

I kept my eyes trained on Mya. It was easier than seeing Nancy's reaction to what she already guessed.

"Sex."

"You mean rape?" Mya said.

Growls rose around me, and Drav quickly held up his hands.

"Mya, I did not growl."

She ignored him and continued to focus on me.

He'd been looking for me for weeks. It couldn't have been easy. An ache built in my chest for his unfailing persistence.

Unable to stop myself, I thought back to the day I'd found the can trail leading to the house with all the food. I recalled the flash of grey and felt a moment of regret. My parents had still been alive. How differently would things have turned out if he had talked to me then? The regret faded as quickly as it had come. Ghua and Mya were right about one thing; if he'd tried that day, he would have been hurt, maybe even have died. I knew without a doubt, the same thing would have still happened to my parents without Ghua there to help us. And I'd be without my parents and Ghua now.

I'd never stop missing my parents, but Ghua made me feel part of something again. We were a team. Sort of. I recalled the way he'd asked me if I wanted to be twelve again, and I knew we were more than a team. I swallowed hard at the tender feelings consuming me and tried focusing on the neighborhood instead.

We walked toward one of the lit-up houses that men were running toward. It looked nice and had solar panels on the roof.

"Off the grid living," Mya said, noting the direction of my scrutiny. "You know, since there's not much of a grid anymore."

"It looks nice."

"Most of the guys here have a house they're working to fix up. We just passed Ghua's," she said, pointing to a cute two-story.

That's when I noticed Ghua was missing. A jolt of panic shot through me.

"Don't worry. He'll be back. He probably went to clean up. I've been drilling it into the fey that they shouldn't touch humans when they have infected blood all over them since we don't know all the ways it might be spread."

"Yeah, he wouldn't carry me when he was bloody."

"Good." She paused walking and turned toward me. "They tend to ask inappropriate questions by our standards and say things that would send my grandma to her grave if she wasn't already dead, but they mean well. They are sincere and loyal and will protect you with their last breath. You don't need to be afraid here."

A large fey came quickly striding up to us. His arms wrapped around Mya from behind, and he hugged her close.

"It is too cold to be outside, Mya."

She grinned at me.

"Eden, this is Drav. My other half."

He glanced at me.

"Hello, Eden."

"Hi."

"It is too cold outside for you, too. Dad has the fire burning, and all the men are in the house to hear your news, Mya."

"Not my news," Mya said, twisting to look up at him. "Eden's news. And, I think you're not going to like hearing it."

He made a soft growly sound as his hard stare locked on me. I was debating if I'd need to run when Mya elbowed him in the ribs. He grunted and looked down at her.

"What did I tell you about growling?" she said. "It's scary. One more growl out of you, and you're sleeping on the couch for a week."

Fifteen

The contrite look on Drav's face was almost comical.

"I am sorry, Eden. I will not growl again." His hold on M tightened, and she patted his arm soothingly while he continu speaking to me. "Come to our house where it is warm. We w listen to your news."

I followed the pair into the crowded house. Heat immediately surrounded me. I would have taken off my jacket, but there was barely walking room with all the bodies crammec into the space.

Despite Mya's assurances that these men were safe, I wished Ghua was with me. The focused way they watched ever move I made unnerved me. With this group, saying I was twelve didn't make me feel safe anymore. Just Ghua did.

Refusing to show my fear, I kept walking as we wove our way into the living room where several other humans sat with Nancy. It looked like she'd pulled herself together a bit. Her eyes were red, but she was no longer crying. One of the fey stood by her. His stance and the way he had more breathing room drew my eyes. He met my gaze and nodded to me.

Mya stopped in the middle of the living room and made introductions.

"Everyone, this is Eden and Nancy. Ladies, this is Molev, the leader of the fey."

"It hasn't been forced yet," I said. "There's been no need. The rations are split equally between the workers and the gunmen, but digging around in the dirt is hungrier work than standing guard. The gunmen are quick to offer their food to the female workers in exchange for whatever the man in question is in the mood for."

"What do we have to worry about the most when we go in for Nancy's kids?" Mya asked.

"The guns, if these guys die from a bullet just like us. The only way in is through a narrow set of stairs leading down. Anyone who's not welcome would be easy to shoot."

"Anything else?"

"Isn't that enough?" Mya's cavalier attitude about the gunmen concerned me. If these guys were as great as she said they were, shouldn't she at least be a little worried that they might get hurt.

"The next hunting party leaves tomorrow morning," Molev said. "They will recover the children instead of hunting the hounds."

Several scattered grunts came from the men in the room.

"Thank you," Nancy said. Her eyes were watering again.

"Hold up," Mya said. "If we're dealing with humans, we need to involve Matt."

"Who's Matt?" Nancy asked.

"He's the leader at Whiteman, the military base not far from here, where the majority of the human survivors live. We're potentially rescuing more than your two kids. If those people don't want to stay here, Whiteman's the only other safe place. Matt needs the heads up."

"We'll speak to Matt first thing in the morning," Molev said with a nod to Mya.

"All right, then. Fey, time to clear out so I can get to bed."

The room quickly emptied; however, Ghua's hands remained on my shoulders, keeping me in place. Not that I had anywhere to go.

With the house void of all the fey but Molev, Drav, and Ghua, Mya looked at me.

"You're welcome to stay here with Nancy and us," she said.

My gaze flicked to Molev, who watched me intently, then at Drav. I didn't like the idea of staying in the same house as either of them when sleeping arrangements already sounded like they would be a little cozy.

"If it's alright with you, I'll stay with Ghua."

He squeezed my shoulders lightly as Mya frowned at me. An older woman, who'd been sitting on the sofa beside Nancy, stood.

"Of course it's all right. I'll walk you there while Ghua takes a minute to chat with Molev about his time away."

"I think I'll come too," Mya said.

"No. You need to get to bed, remember?"

"Mom is correct," Drav said. He scooped Mya up and started down the hall despite her protests.

Mya's mom wrapped her arm through mine and led me to the door.

"I feel like I just missed something," I said once we were outside.

She laughed. "You did. A lecture from my daughter. I'm Julie, by the way. Everyone here tends to just call me Mom."

"Why was I going to hear a lecture?"

"Mya's protective of all the fey. All the humans here are."

I studied her for a moment.

"And you think I'm going to hurt Ghua? Have you seen how

He'd been looking for me for weeks. It couldn't have been easy. An ache built in my chest for his unfailing persistence.

Unable to stop myself, I thought back to the day I'd found the can trail leading to the house with all the food. I recalled the flash of grey and felt a moment of regret. My parents had still been alive. How differently would things have turned out if he had talked to me then? The regret faded as quickly as it had come. Ghua and Mya were right about one thing; if he'd tried that day, he would have been hurt, maybe even have died. I knew without a doubt, the same thing would have still happened to my parents without Ghua there to help us. And I'd be without my parents and Ghua now.

I'd never stop missing my parents, but Ghua made me feel part of something again. We were a team. Sort of. I recalled the way he'd asked me if I wanted to be twelve again, and I knew we were more than a team. I swallowed hard at the tender feelings consuming me and tried focusing on the neighborhood instead.

We walked toward one of the lit-up houses that men were running toward. It looked nice and had solar panels on the roof.

"Off the grid living," Mya said, noting the direction of my scrutiny. "You know, since there's not much of a grid anymore."

"It looks nice."

"Most of the guys here have a house they're working to fix up. We just passed Ghua's," she said, pointing to a cute two-story.

That's when I noticed Ghua was missing. A jolt of panic shot through me.

"Don't worry. He'll be back. He probably went to clean up. I've been drilling it into the fey that they shouldn't touch humans when they have infected blood all over them since we don't know all the ways it might be spread."

"Yeah, he wouldn't carry me when he was bloody."

"Good." She paused walking and turned toward me. "They tend to ask inappropriate questions by our standards and say things that would send my grandma to her grave if she wasn't already dead, but they mean well. They are sincere and loyal and will protect you with their last breath. You don't need to be afraid here."

A large fey came quickly striding up to us. His arms wrapped around Mya from behind, and he hugged her close.

"It is too cold to be outside, Mya."

She grinned at me.

"Eden, this is Drav. My other half."

He glanced at me.

"Hello, Eden."

"Hi."

"It is too cold outside for you, too. Dad has the fire burning, and all the men are in the house to hear your news, Mya."

"Not my news," Mya said, twisting to look up at him. "Eden's news. And, I think you're not going to like hearing it."

He made a soft growly sound as his hard stare locked on me. I was debating if I'd need to run when Mya elbowed him in the ribs. He grunted and looked down at her.

"What did I tell you about growling?" she said. "It's scary. One more growl out of you, and you're sleeping on the couch for a week."

Fifteen

The contrite look on Drav's face was almost comical.

"I am sorry, Eden. I will not growl again." His hold on Mya tightened, and she patted his arm soothingly while he continued speaking to me. "Come to our house where it is warm. We will listen to your news."

I followed the pair into the crowded house. Heat immediately surrounded me. I would have taken off my jacket, but there was barely walking room with all the bodies crammed into the space.

Despite Mya's assurances that these men were safe, I wished Ghua was with me. The focused way they watched every move I made unnerved me. With this group, saying I was twelve didn't make me feel safe anymore. Just Ghua did.

Refusing to show my fear, I kept walking as we wove our way into the living room where several other humans sat with Nancy. It looked like she'd pulled herself together a bit. Her eyes were red, but she was no longer crying. One of the fey stood by her. His stance and the way he had more breathing room drew my eyes. He met my gaze and nodded to me.

Mya stopped in the middle of the living room and made introductions.

"Everyone, this is Eden and Nancy. Ladies, this is Molev, the leader of the fey."

"Tell us who took the children," Molev said, looking at me.

"Men," I said with a shrug, unsure what he was expecting.

"What Molev means is, what can you tell us about the men who took them?"

"Well, there are about twelve gunmen." I frowned. "Maybe less now. Ghua may have killed one of the men who tried to take me back."

"I did not kill him, Mya," Ghua said as he came up behind me and placed his hands on my shoulders.

I exhaled and leaned into his touch a little, feeling calmer and grateful that cleaning up hadn't taken him very long.

"There were eight of us workers before I left. Nine, now, with Nancy's kids," I said with a glance at her. "They are holed up in an underground bunker. There's only one way in, through a steel reinforced door that can lock from the inside. They have a lot of guns and a lot of ammunition and plenty of supplies to last the winter if they chose not to open that door again until spring."

"What are the workers for?" Mya asked.

"Mostly to search the field for forgotten vegetables. Withered, soft, it didn't matter. Fresh food meant not touching the supplies."

"You said mostly. What about when they aren't searching for food?" she asked.

I kept my eyes trained on Mya. It was easier than seeing Nancy's reaction to what she already guessed.

"Sex."

"You mean rape?" Mya said.

Growls rose around me, and Drav quickly held up his hands.

"Mya, I did not growl."

She ignored him and continued to focus on me.

fast he moves? I couldn't touch him if I tried."

"That's where you're wrong." Her voice grew soft, and she looked at me with concern. "For you, he'd hold still. Eden, you have more power to hurt him than anyone else."

Her words made the ache in my chest, the one that had been growing steadily, hurt more.

"He brought you here for a reason. He likes you, Eden. He would do anything for just a pinch of his affection to be returned."

"How can he when he doesn't even know me?" I said, desperate to downplay what I already knew he felt. And, what I already felt myself.

"Ghua left here two weeks ago determined to find you. For a fey, that seems to be more than enough time. It only took Drav a week to learn our language and a good portion of our ways. I think Ghua knows more about you than you realize."

She turned up the sidewalk to the house that Mya had indicated earlier.

"My point is that it would be kinder to tell him now if you will never be romantically interested in return."

I thought of the kiss he and I had shared, and my stomach danced.

"Why do you think I wouldn't be interested?"

She patted my arm and gave me an understanding smile.

"The fey are different. All the women at Whiteman are either married or too afraid of that difference to give them the time of day. However, if you're able to see past Ghua's differences, like Mya did with Drav, then I think you would be interested. Just take some time to get to know Ghua before you decide. And, be honest with him while you're making up your mind."

She opened the door, and I stepped in.

"I'll see you in the morning, Eden."

"Thank you, Julie."

Alone in Ghua's house, I looked around. The entry where I stood opened to the living room and kitchen. To the right, there was a stairway leading to the second floor and a hallway tucked just under the stairs.

The house was warm, smelled clean, and didn't have a single sign of infected occupation. For a few moments, all I could do was stare in envy. Why in the hell had I fought so hard against coming here?

I took my boots off by the door and walked across the pristine carpet toward the stack of movies near the TV. Most of them were chick flicks with a few PG family movies.

Smiling to myself, I tossed aside my jacket and layered shirts until I wore just the farmer's t-shirt. It was easy to get comfortable here. It felt like a real home. I made my way to the couch and sat, ready to enjoy a moment of peace and safety.

Something crinkled under the cushion. I frowned, stood, and lifted the cushion. A pile of nudie magazines waited underneath. I picked the first one up and slowly sat on the neighboring cushion, which also crinkled.

With an aching heart, I opened the magazine promoting the seven guaranteed ways to have the best sex ever. The centerfold was a woman dangling in some swing-type contraption with a man standing between her legs while her ankles were anchored high above.

The front door opened.

I looked up from the magazine. Ghua's gaze flicked from my face to what I read then back to my face. His open, happy expression faded.

I dropped the magazine and stood quickly.

"I changed my mind. I'd like to stay at Mya's house."

Ghua closed the door.

"Wait, Eden." His eyes darted around the room before settling on me, and his grey skin took on a darker hue. "Those aren't mine."

The complete absurdity of his statement robbed me of some of my fear but none of my hurt.

"Right. They just happen to be under the cushions of the couch in the house that belongs to you."

He frowned for a moment. The next words from his mouth weren't the continued denial I was expecting.

"Do humans really have sex in so many ways?"

"What? No. At least, not the average human."

"Why not?"

I picked up the magazine I'd dropped and turned it so he could see the woman strapped in the swing.

"Does that look comfortable to you?"

He looked down at the picture, and his pupils dilated.

"Yes," he said huskily.

My annoyance overrode my verbal filter.

"Stop thinking with your dick and think with your head. Look at her. Look at the way her legs are spread apart and tied to the swing. Would you like to be tied like that?"

He tilted his head.

"No?"

I snorted in disgust and tossed the magazine on the couch.

"Hearing that you'd been looking for me for weeks made me think I might really be something special to you. You said your interest in me wasn't just about sex. Now, I'm not so sure. You said I would be free to leave if I came here. Are you going to let me walk out that door or are you going to stop me?"

He grabbed the back of his neck and growled, clearly frustrated. He paced in front of the door a bit, then looked at me again. Any trace of frustration was gone. Only desperation remained, and that worried me. Desperate people did crazy things.

"Please, Eden. Do not leave me. You are my salvation."

"From what?"

"An eternity of loneliness."

"That sure sounds like a no to letting me leave."

He stalked toward me, making me nervous.

"Stay with me tonight. If you still want to go tomorrow, I will take you to wherever you feel safe."

"I felt safe here until I discovered you have a porn addiction."

"I'm not addicted," he said quickly.

"Oh really?" I turned and flipped all the cushions off the couch to reveal his mountain of magazines.

"That's a shit load of porn for someone who's not addicted to it."

His gaze bounced between me and the porn for several long moments.

"I'll throw it away."

"That won't undo the damage that's already been done."

"What has it damaged?"

"Your mind! Do you seriously think any woman wants to do the stuff that's in these magazines?"

He stared at the couch with remorse.

"They don't?"

"No."

"But Mom said sex is natural."

"Okay, first off, why were you asking Julie about sex? And, second—"

"Mya didn't want to answer our questions anymore," he said quickly. "She does not like the word pussy. Mom says we're just curious, and it's better to get the right information than to guess the wrong thing. Is sex really unnatural?"

The worry in his gaze speared me with guilt and, at the same time, made me want to hug the big idiot. Mya had it right. They asked the most inappropriate questions, but it was because they truly didn't know. The hurt at finding the magazines faded a bit. How could these guys be so smart and so clueless at the same time?

"Sex is natural. But I wouldn't call what's in those magazines sex. Those are models posing for pictures. They are paid to do that."

All expression left his face, and his pupils narrowed to slits.

"Like the men who wanted to give you food for your touch?" he asked softly.

"Yeah. Something like that."

He stepped closer and gingerly wrapped his arms around me.

"I am sorry, my Eden. Forgive me. I did not understand."

His sincerity and gentle hold won me over. I sighed, and hugged his waist in return.

"I know. And I'm sorry if I was starting to yell."

His cheek pressed against the top of my head.

"It's okay. I like when your cheeks are red. It's pretty."

I smiled slightly. He really did make me feel special.

"Can I show you the rest of the house?" he asked.

"Sure."

The house wasn't big (three bedrooms and two bathrooms

upstairs, a living room, kitchen, half bath and laundry downstairs), and the grand tour only took a few minutes. We finished in the kitchen where he opened cupboards full of food options.

I picked out a can of tuna fish and another of peas then sat at the table with him.

"How long have you been living here?" I asked, after eating in silence for a few minutes.

"A few weeks."

So not long before he started looking for me.

"Was all that food here already?"

"No, we've been collecting supplies whenever we go out to hunt the hounds. We give half of what we find to Whiteman and divide the rest."

"How often do you hunt?"

"Molev sends groups out every week. We take turns hunting hounds and helping humans. Mya and Mom said we also needed breaks to rest. I used my rest break to find you."

My heart skipped a beat, and I felt myself falling for him even more.

I got up, rinsed out my cans, and put them in the recycling. The sight of the blue bin made me pause.

"You still recycle?"

"Dad said we shouldn't waste metal because we don't know when we might need it. We're putting the flattened cans in a pile inside the wall."

"Smart."

He rinsed his can and put it in the bin.

"We don't need to be quiet here," he said. "If the hounds come, it makes hunting them easier. You can shower, if you want, or wash your clothes."

My eyes got big at the idea of clean underwear.

"Hell yes."

He smiled slightly, showed me the way to the laundry room, then left me alone. I stripped out of everything but the shirt and threw it all in the washer. With my clothes happily swishing, I went to find Ghua. He was in the living room, gathering all of his magazines, and looked up when I entered. I tried not to fidget when his gaze swept over my bare legs. I'd worn the exact same thing, or lack thereof, before and survived. This time wasn't any different. Except for the fact that he was remorsefully removing his porn collection from the couch cushions.

"Would you like to watch a movie?" he asked.

"If it's okay with you, I think I'm just going to go to bed."

He grunted and went back to his clean up. I escaped upstairs.

All the bedrooms were neat and clean, making it hard to tell which room was his. Without shame, I started looking through dressers. The master bedroom had a few pieces of Ghua-sized clothes in otherwise empty drawers. The dressers in the two other rooms remained empty. The house seemed stripped of any personal items from the previous owners.

Bummed that there wouldn't be any underwear in my near future, I picked one of the guest rooms and pulled back the covers.

No sooner had I settled in than the light turned off.

"You don't need the light on," Ghua said before I could panic that something had happened to the power.

"Oh. Thanks."

The light from outside still made it easy to see, though, and I watched him walk into the room. He took his shirt off, tossed it aside, then started toward me.

"What are you doing?"

"Going to sleep." He lowered himself on the mattress beside me.

"I thought you slept in the big room."

"I did. But if you like this one better, that's okay."

He reached an arm over me in a familiar move. I rolled away, not wanting to get pulled into Ghua snuggle time.

However, instead of escaping, I rolled my chest right into his palm. We both froze. His fingers moved, gently squeezing my breast, then slowly lifting away. A fingertip dragged against my nipple. It didn't feel wrong at all. In fact, it felt so right a sound escaped me.

"Did I hurt you?" he asked.

"No."

His hand immediately returned and stroked my nipple again. The heat of his fingers branded my skin and started a slow burn in my middle. I groaned and quickly turned toward him, dislodging his touch. This connection between us felt too new and unsure—especially given my recent discovery—to jump into something physical, no matter what my body was telling me.

Looking up, I opened my mouth to try to explain. I never got the chance to utter a word.

Ghua's fingers curled around the back of my neck a moment before his mouth covered mine in a searing kiss so hot it made my toes curl. Every reason why I should say no fled my mind with the swipe of his tongue against mine. I lifted my hands and buried my fingers in his hair.

He growled into my mouth, and his hand stroked up my side, unerringly finding my breast again. His fingers played with my hard nipple. I pulled away with a gasp.

Undeterred, he trailed kisses along my throat.

"My Eden," he whispered. "My perfect Eden."

Julie's warning and Mya's words circled in my mind.

"Ghua, stop," I panted.

He lifted his head and looked at me, his pupils very large in the dim light.

"This is going too fast. I didn't mean to lead you on or make you think I'm ready for sex. I liked kissing you, but I'm terrified of more. I don't want what you've seen in those magazines. Honestly, I don't know what I do want."

He reached up and smoothed a hand over my hair.

"You liked kissing me?" he asked quietly.

"Yes."

"Your heart is racing. Did my touch scare you?"

"No." I swallowed hard and forced the truth out. "It's racing because the way you touched me felt really good."

He grabbed my shoulders and flipped us so I was laying under him. Before I could panic, he looked me in the eyes.

"Tell me how old you are, Eden."

Heart still pounding and my breast tingling from where he'd touched it, I stared up at him. My stomach went hot and cold as I realized what he was asking.

"I don't know," I whispered, fighting the fear creeping up my spine.

He leaned forward and brushed his nose against mine.

"You do know. Stop being afraid, Eden. Trust me to care for you."

Could I trust him? Maybe. Because right now, when he so easily could, he wasn't taking or forcing; he was letting me choose.

I closed my eyes and whispered the words that would seal my fate.

“I’m nineteen.”

Sixteen

Ghua rolled us to our sides and wrapped an arm around my waist to pull me flush with his chest. I forced myself to relax and waited for what he'd do next. The gentle brush of his nose against mine surprised me. As did the fingers running through my hair. I'd thought he would go back to my chest, or worse, under my shirt to discover I wasn't wearing any underwear.

He held me close and placed small kisses on my temple and brow. Then he exhaled in his contented way, and the movement of his fingers began to slow. He was falling asleep. What I felt for the man holding me intensified, and I grinned.

Warm, safe, and comfortable, it didn't take me long to fall asleep, too.

Before meeting Ghua, most of my nights were spent sleeping in short bursts, waking from dreams filled with my struggles to kill infected before I became one myself. Those dreams had faded, replaced with real sleep and dreams I never remembered when waking.

Until now.

I'd been dreaming of Ghua kissing his way up from my bellybutton when the ache he'd created became real. Opening my eyes, I blinked at the wall of chiseled chest inches from my face.

The stroke of Ghua's thumb over my nipple kindled the

already slow burn between my legs, and I fought not to arch into his hand. I could only guess how long he'd been touching me. The thought had barely surfaced before another took its place. His thumb was directly caressing skin. No shirt barrier.

That meant he knew I had nothing else on. The ache turned into a throb.

I tilted my head to meet his gaze.

"Is it time to wake up?" I asked, struggling to distract myself.

"Almost." The sound of his husky voice made the heat in my middle climb higher.

His nose nuzzled mine, and he pressed a light kiss on my upper lip.

"We should get up." I sounded breathless and unsure. Damn.

"Just a few more minutes."

He flattened his palm over my breast and began to gently knead it. I gave in and arched into his touch with a groan.

He growled, set his forehead to mine, and continued his exploration of the size and feel of my left breast. And it didn't scare me in the least. I closed my eyes and enjoyed the moment, taking it for myself like the first time I'd slept next to him.

It felt good to be touched. To not be afraid. To think of something other than the world outside.

I put my hand on his side, letting my fingers learn the smooth, hard texture of his skin. Unable to resist, I trailed them to his stomach and traced each defined ab. He twitched under my touch, and his breathing grew ragged.

I opened my eyes and met his hot stare.

"I think we should stop," I said softly.

His hand stilled.

"Will you touch me again?" His voice was hoarse with need.

"Maybe. If you don't get mad that I want to stop now."

He placed a kiss on the corner of my mouth then the tip of my nose.

"I am grateful for what you've given me. I would never be angry."

I'd let him cop a feel. While I didn't think it was much, he obviously did.

He moved his hand and reverently tugged my shirt back into place. I watched him for a moment, my head wrestling with my heart. My heart was winning big time.

"Thank you, Ghua."

"For what?"

"For listening when I said stop. For not being angry. For helping me feel safe."

"I told you, I will protect you."

And now I understood what he meant. He'd protect me from everything, even himself. I sat up, my heart melting a good deal as I studied him.

"You were purposely looking for me. Why? What is it you want from me?" I asked.

"Mya said that people who are married have given a promise to never leave each other. I want you to promise to stay with me, Eden."

I could only stare at him. Had he just proposed to me? The complete devotion in his eyes and the way he gently reached out to stroke my cheek said he had. And he knew it.

In a state of numbed shock, I climbed over him to get out of bed.

"I need to take a shower before we go."

Without looking back, I walked down to the master suite where I knew the bathroom had towels.

Why was I so shocked? Because a proposal had been the last thing I'd thought he'd say. Given the porn, I'd thought he'd ask for a blowjob or something. I'd been prepared to maybe play around a little more. Ghua wasn't playing, though. At least not the way I'd been willing to play. He wanted for keeps. In this world? Was he insane? No, he wasn't human.

While my thoughts whirled, I started the shower to let the water warm.

Ghua didn't understand what he was asking. He couldn't. Could he? Maybe. He wanted me to trust him for life. What should have been a good thing, actually freaked me out more. While I now trusted him to keep me safe and not use me for sex, I was still living in one day at a time mode. He was asking me to not do that. He was asking me to think of the future. He was asking me to let go of all my fears. But, he didn't understand what that meant. It wasn't just about me putting my life in his hands. It was trusting that he would stay alive, too.

Would that trust be so hard to give, though? I mean, he didn't have to worry about survival to the level that I did. He was strong and fast and bigger than life. He fought infected like it was nothing. Their bites didn't make him sick. If I could trust anyone to stay alive in this world with me, it was Ghua.

I rubbed a hand over my face and pulled my shirt over my head.

"I don't understand what I did wrong," Ghua said from behind me.

I yipped and grabbed the towel to wrap around me. He wasn't looking at my body, though. He was looking at my face, his expression confused and a bit upset.

"I did not ask for sex from you."

"I know, Ghua. You asked for something a lot more."

"I don't understand," he repeated.

"You're asking for my heart and my trust. It would have been easier if you'd just asked for my body."

"I want that too," he said quickly, as if afraid he might miss out if he didn't speak up, "but I would like your heart and trust first."

I smiled slightly, unable to help myself, and walked up to him.

"I know what you want from me now." I stood on my toes and kissed him lightly on the lips. "I just need some time to wrap my head around my life and all the changes in the last few days."

"You're not angry?"

"No."

He exhaled heavily and grabbed the back of my head to press his forehead to mine.

"Good."

I wrapped my arms around his waist and hugged him hard. He shuddered.

"You really like it when I touch you, don't you."

"More than anything."

My heart skipped a beat. I ached to give him what he wanted. Real, tangible affection. I lifted my head, looked back at the glass enclosed shower that was filling with steam, then up at Ghua.

"The shower looks big enough to fit two. Want me to wash your back?"

A wide grin split his face.

"Yes."

Before I could blink, he pulled out of my arms and had his pants around his ankles. I stared open mouthed at the erection rising thick and long from his pelvis.

"Are you going to shower with your towel on?" he asked.

I blinked at him and noticed the sly, teasing look in his eyes.

"Are we playing the 'I'll show you mine if you show me yours' game?" I asked.

"That sounds fun. How do we play?"

I let my towel drop to the floor. His gaze traced down the length of me with slow fascination. By the time he reached my toes, my cheeks felt like they were on fire.

"What are the rules?" he asked, meeting my gaze again. "Am I allowed to touch you?"

"Yes. Unless I ask you to stop."

He grunted and nodded, his gaze drifting to my breasts. His erection bounced as he studied them.

"Am I allowed to kiss you?" he asked.

"Yes."

His hand went to his shaft. He idly stroked it as his gaze dipped lower. My pulse jumped nervously, and my bravado began to fade.

"Am I allowed to—"

"Maybe this isn't a good idea."

His gaze flew to mine, and he released himself.

"No. This is a good idea. You will wash my back. I will wash you. Then, we will leave for Whiteman. I will follow the rules. I will stop washing when you say stop."

I considered him for a moment then nodded. Without waiting to see what he'd do or ask next, I turned and walked toward the shower. A low growl rumbled behind me, and I glanced over my shoulder. His gaze was fixated on my ass.

I stopped walking and motioned for him to get in first. He dutifully complied and faced the spray, tall enough that it wasn't hitting him in the face.

As he stood waiting, I found myself looking at him with the same interest he'd looked at me. He had a nice butt. Tight and nicely rounded. Not a speck of hair on it, unlike all the butts I'd seen at the bunker. I shook the thought from my head and reached for the body soap.

He shuddered again at the first touch of my hand on his shoulders and reached out to brace a hand on the wall. I smoothed my palm over the broad planes of his back not just washing but rubbing, too. He groaned, letting me know just how much he liked it.

When I got to his hips, his other hand slapped against the glass.

"You okay?" I asked. "Want me to stop?"

"Please do not stop." His voice came out strained and husky.

I brushed my hands over the globes of his butt, circling and testing the feel of him as I created a layer of bubbles. The sound of his ragged breaths filled the shower.

Conflicted thoughts warred in my mind as I stared at his hands gripping the walls as if he was holding on for life. I was playing with fire. What if this went too far? Was I willing to go all the way? No. At least, not yet. But, I wasn't willing to stop either.

When he'd looked at me with hunger before we'd started this, it had made me nervous and quick to want to pull away. It shouldn't have. He'd proven himself time and again. I could trust him not to push for more than I was willing to give. And, hearing him now, desperately trying to hold himself together, drove me to want to do wicked things despite the whispers of caution in my head.

Biting my lip, I slipped my hand over his hip. He tensed and stopped breathing. I slid my hand across his abs and down toward his pelvis. My fingers closed over him, and he made a pained sound. I stroked up his length, marveling and fearing just how much there was.

His head fell forward, and he jerked into my palm. I stepped closer, my breasts brushing against his no longer soapy back, so I could use my other hand too. His breath hissed out of him the moment I gently cupped his balls.

He arched forward into the downward stroke of my hand on his shaft, and I pressed my lips to his back. Another shudder ran through him. I squeezed him when I reached the base then started back up, increasing speed. He growled when I reached the tip and squeezed, and he thrust forward, demanding more. I gave it. His scrotum tightened within seconds.

I knew he was close but didn't expect the roar that came from him as he flung his head back and arched into my hand. I pressed another kiss to his back and didn't stop until his shaft finished jerking.

He turned lightning fast and lifted me high against the wall, his expression fierce.

"My Eden," he growled.

Before I could guess his intent, he shoved his face between my legs.

"St-ah!"

His tongue lapped over the length of my seam, parting me just over my clit. I bucked and gripped his hair. His mouth closed over the sensitive swell, and for the next several minutes, I hung on for dear life.

The orgasm that exploded through me tunneled my vision and robbed me of thought. An inarticulate stream of words poured out of me with each wave. Ghua's tongue didn't still until my head fell back against the wall. He pressed a kiss to my clit, which made me twitch, then gently lowered me.

He held me tightly in his arms and smoothed his hand over my back.

"I did not break the rules," he said firmly. "That was a kiss. Can we play again?"

I lifted my head enough to blink up at him, still barely able to stand if not for his hold. His strong jaw and the determined, heated look in his eyes sent a throb of desire between my legs again.

"I don't think I can. My legs are too shaky."

He grunted and turned off the water. Keeping me steady with one arm, he reached out the door for the towel.

"I didn't get to wash my hair," I protested weakly.

"We will wash it when your legs no longer shake."

He started to dry me carefully, but I stole the towel when he reached my sensitive breasts. He grunted and surrendered the towel to get his own. While he was still drying, I grabbed my shirt and slipped from the bathroom.

This time through the room, I saw my clothes neatly laid out on the bed.

"I dried them for you," he said, coming up behind me.

"Thanks." Heat crept into my cheeks. Why was I blushing?

"I put a toothbrush in the bathroom for you, too."

I should have turned and thanked him again. Instead, I stayed facing the bed, unsure and a bit embarrassed.

"There is powdered milk and cereal in the kitchen. Mya said that humans like it."

"We do."

"I will wait for you downstairs."

His lips pressed against the back of my head, then he was

gone.

I covered my face with my hands.

What the hell did I just do?

Seventeen

I could feel Ghua's gaze on me, but I didn't look up from my bowl of cereal. Guilt and nerves kept my head down.

I hadn't thought things would go so far. After Ghua had asked me to spend my life with him, I only wanted to escape so I could give myself some time to think. The last thing I should have done was entice him to shower with me when my mind was still in a jumble about how to answer him. Yet, I'd liked every bit of what we'd done. Did I want more? Hell, yes. But, should I? Leading him on and making him think I would stay wasn't right. Would I stay? My heart was screaming yes, and my mind couldn't think of any reason I shouldn't. I blamed my conflict on Ghua. I could barely remember how I was supposed to view the world anymore. It was supposed to be scary, but it didn't feel that way. Not with him around. That was a problem, wasn't it?

"I don't like this," Ghua said, frustration in his voice.

I looked up at him, confused. He wasn't eating the cereal, I was. He had a can of spam. For breakfast. Dawn's early light was just brightening the sky outside.

"You don't like what?"

"You thinking."

"Excuse me?"

"You don't talk when you think. You won't look at me, and you make angry faces at your food. You are not happy when you think. Stop thinking. Let's go play our game again. You were happy playing our game."

"Ghua, I—"

A knock on the front door saved me.

He grunted and went to answer it, clearly annoyed.

"Morning, Ghua," Mya said. Drav stood just behind her. "You guys ready?"

"Almost," I said, lifting my bowl and gulping the milk Ghua had made for me. It was the first milk I'd had in weeks and tasted amazing. I wasn't about to waste it.

Chewing the last few bits of cereal, I took my bowl to the sink and made to wash it.

"Leave it," Mya said. "I'll come back later and clean up."

"You're not going with us?" The way she'd spoken last night, it had sounded like she would.

"No. I've been placed under house arrest by the overprotective pain in the butt standing behind me."

"Mya," Drav said in a warning tone.

She rolled her eyes at me.

"Molev's waiting by the wall. So are the rest of the fey."

Drav and Mya walked with us to the wall. Nancy was already there, held in the arms of the same man who had held her last time. Without warning, Ghua scooped me up, too.

"If you find any peanut butter cups out there, bring them back for me," Mya called as Ghua climbed up and over the wall.

After that, I tucked my face against Ghua's chest to avoid the wind.

* * * *

Whiteman wasn't quite what I'd expected. After seeing Ghua's home, I'd thought it would be something similar. However, the base looked nothing like the well-protected, cozy neighborhood. A metal, barbwire-topped fence stretched far in both directions. Every one hundred or so feet, there was a makeshift tower with a light. Every other tower had an armed guard. Directly inside the fence, there was nothing but a large field of dormant grass. Further in, I could see a few white buildings and trees.

"We're here to see Matt Davis," Molev called to the guard. The first gate swung open, and our group crowded in.

"Can I get down, now?" I asked after almost kicking one of the other fey in the side.

Ghua's hold on me tightened fractionally, and he glanced up at the armed guard staring down at us.

"Not yet."

I didn't argue. The first gate closed behind us and the second one swung open. The fey jogged across the grass and tarmac toward one of the large, white buildings. As we approached, a door opened and a man walked out.

"Molev," the man said with a nod. "I wasn't expecting to see you, but I'm glad you've come. I wanted to personally thank you for the supplies you've been sending with your men. Without your help, we would have never lasted this long."

Molev grunted in acknowledgement, which made me smile. Noncommittal grunting seemed to be a fey thing.

"Matt, this is Nancy. Her children were taken from her by a group of humans. They mean to force her daughter to have sex."

Matt's eyes widened, and he looked at Nancy. Surprisingly, today, she was holding herself together.

"It's true," she said. "My daughter's seventeen, and my son's fifteen. The men who took them killed my husband. Eden knows where they are."

"We're on our way to get them back," Molev said. "There

are other humans being kept, too. Mya thought you should know because they might want to return with us and stay here."

"Yes. Of course. We'll welcome them all. We need the help after the last attack."

"What attack?" I asked.

"Infected found a way in the fence, and we lost a dozen of our people. We have guards posted around the entire perimeter now. It's a very large area to protect. We're running four-hour alternating shifts. People are getting tired. More survivors will be very welcomed."

He glanced at Molev, "If you're open to the help, I have a truck I can send with you so you don't need to carry the survivors back."

Molev started to shake his head. Nancy, who couldn't see him from her position in Kerr's arms, spoke before Molev could.

"Thank you," Nancy said. "That would be very much appreciated."

Molev met Matt's glance and gave a single nod.

"It will take me a little bit of time to ask for volunteers and rearrange the schedules," Matt said. "I'll start on it immediately. You're welcome to use whatever facilities you want while you wait."

"Thank you, Matt Davis." Molev didn't sound surprised exactly. More like unsure.

He watched Matt retreat into the white building once more then looked at his men.

"Meet back here in an hour," Molev said.

Ghua looked down at me.

"Would you like to see Whiteman?"

"Sure."

He split off from the group, walking north.

"You going to carry me the whole time?"

He grinned.

"If you'll let me."

"I'd prefer to walk. My legs are starting to hurt."

He quickly set me down. Side by side, we walked through the base. He pointed out what each of the buildings was used for, the derelict houses where no one wanted to stay, and the tent community back by the trees and fence.

"I'd pick a house over a tent any day," I said. "Why are they living like this?"

"Fear."

I snorted.

"That's why I'd live in a house. There's no way that a tent would keep an infected out." I didn't mention the hellhounds because we both knew houses wouldn't keep them out, either.

"It's the fear of how close the houses are to the fence and what happened in the houses. When the hellhounds first came, the people in the town were infected and came here. The humans had many guns. They eventually killed all the infected, but many of the houses were shot in the process. Windows are broken. Walls have holes in them. The survivors did not want the reminder of what had happened. The tents make them feel safer because they are closer together and further away from town where any noise they make might draw more infected."

He stopped in front of a tent close to the fence.

"I wouldn't feel safe here," I said.

"This is where I lived before we moved to Tolerance."

He pulled the flap aside, and I stepped in. Before I could see much, the flap closed behind us, pitching the interior into darkness. A lamp flared a moment later.

Three cots hugged the three walls. Each had a single

blanket and no pillow. There was no woodstove like I'd noticed in many of the tents further from the fence, and out of the daylight it felt colder.

"I bet you're glad you don't have to sleep on these cots anymore."

"I still stay here when it's my turn to help at Whiteman. We don't sleep much, though. The humans like our help."

"How often do you come here?"

"About twice a month."

"For how long?"

"A few days."

"A few days without heat or decent sleep?" I'd been in that position before and knew it sucked big time. "We need to fix this place up for you or you're going to get sick."

I shivered and hugged myself. Ghua immediately stepped closer and wrapped his arms around me. His body heat made all the difference.

"I don't get sick like you do, and this is more than I had in Ernisi."

How could this be more? What had he slept on? Rocks?

His words about an eternity of loneliness took on a deeper meaning. He'd literally had nothing before coming here.

"I think we should head back," I said.

He grunted but didn't let go. I tipped my head back against his chest to look up at him. His gaze dipped to my mouth. Slowly, he lowered his head. My pulse jumped at the first touch of his lips.

He took his time, kissing me slowly. When he finally pulled back, I was breathless and my knees were weak.

The yearning look he gave me reminded me that I still hadn't given him an answer. Julie told me not to string him along, and I wasn't. At least, not intentionally. I'd just spent too long living in the moment to think about the future like he wanted me to. I needed more time.

"We should head back," I repeated.

He didn't look disappointed, but I couldn't help but imagine that's what he felt as he kissed my forehead then swung me up into his arms. I didn't like disappointing Ghua.

* * * *

The truck rumbled along the road. Ahead, Ghua ran with several other fey and moved cars out of the way. They also cleared any infected trying to hide in the vehicles.

"This sure beats how we traveled to the base," Nancy said from beside me.

Warm inside the cab of the big utility truck, I watched Ghua run tirelessly for another moment and looked at her.

"For us, maybe. Not for them." We'd been driving for several hours. Because of the fey running ahead, we hadn't needed to stop like on the way to the base. While it would get us to the old man's house faster, which is where Ghua was leading us, it also meant the fey hadn't had a break since we started.

"How do you know when to stop so they can rest?" I asked the driver, who'd introduced himself as Will.

Not only was I worried Ghua and the other fey would tire themselves, I was missing Ghua.

Will shrugged. "We've never had to stop. I think they're used to running like this."

"I was used to being harassed and starved, but does that make it right to keep harassing and starving me?"

The guy gave me a surprised look but immediately slowed down. Ghua ran back to us as we came to a stop, and I rolled down my window.

"Would you guys like to rest a bit? Maybe eat or drink something?" I asked.

"No. We are almost there. I think we will be able to reach your bunker before dark."

"Okay. If you're sure."

He smiled slightly and nodded. "We are fine, my Eden. Thank you for thinking of us."

He patted the truck then ran ahead once more. Will didn't say anything as he started forward.

Although nothing looked familiar to me, I didn't doubt that we were close. Ghua had a freakishly amazing sense of direction, which I'd witnessed on the way to Tolerance. And it wasn't because he had a great memory for road signs because he couldn't read.

When we pulled into the driveway of the old man's place, I was quick to call a stop.

"There's glass further ahead. We should walk from here."

Nancy waited with Will while the fey and a few of the human men followed me. The house still looked boarded up like when we'd left it. Except no old man threatened us with a gun as we approached. I knocked on the door and waited for several minutes before turning the knob. Ghua put his hand over mine and stopped me from opening the door.

"I will check the house," he said. "You stay with Kerr."

"Check the little door in the pink room upstairs. They might be in there."

"They?"

"There was a young girl in there last time."

He nodded and didn't comment about me not telling him about the girl until now. I stood in the yard while Ghua checked the house.

"There's no one here," he said after he returned. "It looks like the old man and the girl packed up and left. None of the windows are broken, and there were no infected inside."

I hoped that meant they'd made it somewhere safe.

We got back in the truck and made our way to the house where Ghua had found me. From there, it wasn't hard for me to point the way to the bunker.

We arrived at the unpleasantly familiar entrance just before dusk.

Van's truck and an extra car waited not far from the bunker door. Light already shone through the small portal, a sure sign they'd bedded in for the night.

"Okay," I said, getting out of the truck. "What's the plan? How are we going to get in?

Ghua came over and took my hand.

"Do you trust me...us...to keep you safe?"

I stared up at him and felt torn between amusement and nerves.

"You want me to knock on the door, don't you?"

"I want you to stand in front of the door and let me knock on it."

It would work. The men would open the door once they saw me. What would happen afterward, though, worried me.

"Don't forget that they have guns."

"We will not forget."

I stared at him a moment, my fear riding me.

"I'm trusting you to stay alive, Ghua," I said softly.

He pulled me into his arms and hugged me close. The press of his lips to my forehead comforted me more than any words could have.

Sighing, I pulled away with one last look at him, then went

over to the door and stood in front of it. Molev and Ghua stood on each side of the door. The rest of the men stood off to the sides, ready to rush forward.

I nodded to Ghua. He pounded on the door three times.

Despite the cold, my palms grew sweaty while we waited. The light in the sky faded further. I was just about to take a step forward to peer through the portal when I caught a shadow of movement.

Van's face appeared. He looked at me, a slow smile lifting his lips.

"It's Eden. I can't believe you're still alive," he said, his words barely discernable through the thick door.

"I'm alive but won't be for long if you don't let me in."

He grinned wider.

"Déja vu, don't you think?"

"Just let me in, Van."

"You want in? Show me your tits. And that's just a down payment for what you'll owe me."

A faint growl rose from both Molev and Ghua, and I remembered the stern scolding Ghua had given when I'd flashed him. He'd told me not to show my boobs to anyone. Granted, he'd seen them when we'd showered and hadn't seemed to mind. A flush rose to my cheeks as I recalled that enjoyable experience. What I needed to do now would be far from enjoyable, though. If I lifted my shirt, we'd get in, and we'd likely get Nancy's kids. However, when I lifted my shirt, I'd be flashing Van, Ghua, and Molev. I was only okay with one of those three seeing what I had.

I grabbed the bottom of my shirt. Ghua started waving wildly. I looked around, as if checking for infected, and saw that all the other fey were turning around. When I focused on the door once more, Molev had his eyes closed and Ghua looked ready to rip someone's head off.

"You're a dick, Van. And, someday, someone bigger is going to come along and kick your ass for it."

I lifted my shirt and at the same time pulled the sport bra above my boobs. I counted to three, so Van would be good and distracted by thoughts of what he imagined us doing once he let me in, then tugged my clothes back into place.

Van's eager gaze remained fixed on me as the door unlocked.

Molev opened his eyes and looked at Ghua. Even without shifting my focus from Van's eager face, I caught the unnaturally dark hue of Ghua's normal grey tone.

The handle moved, and the door groaned as it swung open. Ghua tensed. As soon as the gap was large enough for Ghua's arm, he reached in and grabbed Van by the throat. Van's eyes bulged. Before he could make a sound, Ghua pulled him from the protection of the bunker.

Around us, the men rushed forward and began their silent entry. At least half their number stayed above. Ignoring them, I looked at the man who'd tormented me for weeks.

"Van, let me introduce you to someone bigger. Now, take it like a man."

Ghua slammed his fist into Van's face, and I heard crunching. Van opened his mouth and let out a yell, which Ghua quickly muffled.

"I will leave you out here with any infected you call," he warned.

Van sobbed quietly, but Ghua didn't release him.

"No female will ever be yours. You are unworthy."

I couldn't have agreed more.

A few shouts came from below but no gunfire. Molev's voice echoed up the steps.

"Bring everyone in. We will stay here for the night. Nancy's children are waiting for her."

Ghua shifted his hold on Van and walked him down the stairs by the back of his neck. I followed, grinning the whole way. When I reached the bottom, each gunman was either on the floor unconscious or being held by a fey. All of my former captors were bleeding. I even saw Steve and Ty. The fey were completely unscathed. I didn't feel an ounce of remorse for my part in helping the fey get in.

Will whistled low when he passed the cage that held all the supplies.

Moving further into the bunker, I found a familiar scene in the kitchen area. May and the rest of the workers were either sitting at the table or waiting to be served by Oscar, who still held the ladle as he watched me approach.

While most of them looked terrified, including the two new kids, Oscar's eyes held a hint of calculation. Unlike the rest of the gunmen, he hadn't been attacked nor was he being held by the fey. Without a gun, Oscar looked like one of the captives, not the lead captor.

"Oscar," I said, retaining my smile. "It's not good to see you. I rather hoped you'd died a painful death by now."

That got every nearby fey's attention.

Ghua, who still held Van by the scruff of the neck, glanced at me.

"Who is this man?"

"He is the leader of the gunmen and Van's father."

"Is he a bigger dick than Van?" Ghua asked.

"Not bigger. Just smarter."

Oscar's gaze flicked to his son. He set down his ladle then held my gaze.

"What is it you want from us, Eden?"

"Your workers and half the supplies."

Van started making angry noises, which Ghua stopped with a firmer grip.

"What if the workers don't want to leave?" Oscar asked.

I looked at the faces I knew.

"There's a military base a day's drive from here. There's at least five hundred human survivors there. They're working together. Real equality, not this bullshit. And, these other guys, the fey, help keep those humans safe in exchange for nothing."

Someone made a sound of disbelief.

"No one does something for nothing."

I nodded slowly. "I know. Humans don't do things for nothing. These guys aren't human. They're nicer. By a lot."

"Prove it," May said.

I glanced at the fey around me.

"Anyone here want to see my boobs? All you have to do is feed me in exchange for a peek."

Eighteen

A chorus of, "No, Eden," filled the bunker along with Ghua's stern, "No one may see your boobs. I will feed you without looking."

May blinked at the men and said nothing more.

"No one's going to force any of you to leave. If you really want to stay with these shitbags, that's on you. If you want to try it on your own, which I wouldn't recommend because the infected are getting smarter, you can take a portion of the supplies tomorrow morning and go whichever way the wind takes you. Or you can take a chance that what I'm saying is true, that there are survivors out there working together, and you can leave with us at first light. There's a truck outside to take us back to the base."

As if mentioning the truck had conjured Nancy, the bodies parted to let Kerr through. He once again carried Nancy in his arms. The moment she saw her children, she started sobbing. The kids jumped up and ran to her.

The heartfelt reunion was short lived, though.

"What about them?" Nancy asked. "What about the men who killed my husband? What happens to them?"

"What do you want to happen to them?" I asked.

"I want them to pay."

"You mean kill them?"

Nancy's hard gaze met mine, and I knew that was exactly what she wanted. I looked at my tormentors. Half of them glared back at me. Half looked remorseful. None of how they felt now, though, could change their past actions. Nothing could. The past was past.

"Killing them won't bring your husband back. It will, however, reduce the healthy human population by a few more. Yes, we both know these guys really don't add any value to that number, but given all the infected and hellhounds out there, it's a number we need to hold onto if we can. Plus, I don't think you want their deaths on your head, Nancy. You don't want to be like them."

She looked away, her eyes filling with tears.

"Thank you, Eden," Oscar said.

"Shut up, Oscar. I'm not standing up for you. I'm standing up for her. Now, hand over the supply keys."

"Why?"

"Because these guys haven't eaten since breakfast and ran the whole way here. They need food."

"It comes out of your half," he said, fishing the end of the necklace that held the keys out of his shirt.

"You're in no position to make the rules anymore."

"We always treated you fairly."

"Really? Except for that whole keeping me against my will thing and wanting to use me as a breeder for the next generation of your sick little family, right?"

He deadeyed me as he threw the keys. Ghua caught them and glanced at me. Since arriving, all the fey had let me do the talking. I wasn't fooled by their silence, though. They knew exactly what was going on and who the bad guys were. They were just letting me deal with it until I needed their help, just like

Ghua had done since the moment he'd found me.

"Go ahead and get something to eat," I said.

I looked at Nancy and her kids. Brenna, Nancy's daughter, clung to her mom's hand. I had no idea what had happened to her while here and knew that Nancy probably wanted a private moment to find out those details.

"There's a room that way with beds in it. Why don't you and your kids take a few minutes while these guys eat?"

Nancy nodded, grateful, and Kerr started toward the room I'd indicated.

Ghua glanced at Oscar before releasing Van. I knew Ghua didn't want to let him go with me standing so near. So, I picked up a knife from the counter, something I'd dreamt of doing while living here.

"Go," I said. "I'll be fine."

Ghua stepped closer to me and pressed his forehead to mine, then walked back toward the food cage. I wasn't left alone, though. Several fey lingered nearby. How could they not? The bunker wasn't huge, and we'd just stuffed an extra sixty bodies into it. I put the knife aside, knowing I wouldn't need it with so many of them around.

"Are you really with one of those things? Do you even know what they are?"

Van's nasally voice made me smile slightly as I answered.

"Yes, I know what they are. They are fey, who have lived thousands of years and were released from their prison along with the hellhounds."

"Imprisoned fey? You can't honestly be siding with them over your own kind," Oscar said softly, his gaze going to the nearest fey.

"And you think you're my kind?"

"You know what he means, Eden," Van said. "You could have been with me. I might still let you."

"I have zero interest in being with you. Ever. When are you going to get that through your thick head?"

"You'd rather be with the grey monster that just touched you? It looked pretty cozy. We both know I'm a better option."

I made a sound of amused disbelief.

"Oh, Van. There's no way you could ever hope to compete with him. He's stronger, smarter, kinder, and hung like a horse. Seriously. Like this big." I held up my hands like I was showing the fish I'd caught. "Your pathetic excuse for a pole is laughable in comparison."

He flushed.

"Is that all you want? A big dick?"

His hate-filled tone and gaze didn't bother me. Yet, my taunting grin faded.

"All I've ever wanted was to feel safe and respected."

"Me too," May said from the table, reminding me that our conversation was far from private.

A few other workers made sounds of agreement.

I met Oscar's expressionless gaze.

"I don't think anyone's going to be staying with you," I said. "Have fun getting your own supplies."

I turned and went to find Ghua. He stood by the supply cage, passing cans of meat out. Ty had regained his feet and his attitude.

"You can't just take all the meat," he said, glaring at me.

"What, isn't this the code you live by? If you want something, take it? Doesn't feel so good to be the suppressed and downtrodden, does it?"

"Is that why you're doing this? Revenge?"

I studied him for a minute, remembering how he'd hit me with the butt of his gun.

"If you hadn't taken those kids, I probably would have never come back. But I had to, and I'm doing my best to make it fun for me. So, is this about revenge? Hell, yeah."

He drew back to spit at me. A fey stepped between us so quickly I had barely registered the move before I heard a crack. Ty swore. When the fey stepped back again, Ty was holding his cheek.

"No spitting," the fey warned.

I grinned and turned my back on Ty. Ghua stood just behind me, two cans of food in his hands. His gaze swept over my face. I wasn't sure what he was looking for, but he seemed to not like what he saw because he frowned at me and stepped closer.

"We will leave at first light," he said. "You will never need to come here again."

My heart warmed that he understood my hate of this place. Wrapping my arms around his waist, I hugged him close.

"Thank you."

He pressed his lips to the top of my head.

"Fucking disgusting," Ty said. "What a waste."

Ghua pulled back to look at me. This time I knew he was looking for a reaction to Ty's harsh words.

"I don't think he learned any respect with just one slap," I said. "Oh, and he's the one who bruised my head."

Ghua grunted and looked over my shoulder. This time a thunk rang out in the air, and I grinned.

"Come, Eden."

Ghua took my hand and led me toward the kitchen where we both grabbed a fork to eat our tins of tuna. Oscar and Van glared at me from their positions as if I were the bad guy here. I didn't feel a pinch of remorse eating the supplies that I'd risked my life for time and again while they stood by with their guns.

Before we finished eating, the other workers quietly got up, one by one, and left the area. All of the workers headed toward the room with the beds. Routines never died, it seemed. Not even during a liberation.

The other fey ate, too. Most of them consumed their canned meat of choice while standing in whatever space they could find. Once everyone finished, most of the fey got comfortable sitting against a wall or laying on the cold cement floor. A few remained alert and watched over the gunmen. But, without their guns, they didn't pose much of a threat.

I set my can aside and tossed my fork into the sink. I didn't wash it. Whoever decided to stay could do that tomorrow.

Ghua sat against the wall in the kitchen and motioned for me. I moved to sit beside him, but he pulled me into his lap at the last second. I didn't try to pull away. The floor was hard and cold, and Ghua was warm and comfortable. Snuggling against him, I closed my eyes.

* * * *

The loud baying of hounds penetrated the fog of my sleep. Yelling and screaming broke out. The sounds layered over one another to create a chaotic racket. I forced my eyes open and tried to understand what was happening in the bunker's dim, red emergency lighting.

The fey who'd settled in near us had already jumped to their feet and were rushing toward the stairwell door. Ghua shifted me off his lap onto the floor. Before I could ask what was going on, he moved to block the kitchen's only entry point.

Grunts and growls filled the air.

"Stop the second one," someone yelled.

Second one? Another howl filled the air, and I scrambled to my feet, realizing what was happening. Somehow, the hounds had gotten in.

Ghua looked back at me.

"I will keep you—"

Something dark flew over the top of the fey in front of him and barreled right into Ghua's chest. He staggered back a single step from the impact then grabbed for the thing made of nightmares. A hellhound.

I stared in horror as the hound's massive jaw clamped down on Ghua's forearm. Ghua grunted and wrapped his other arm around the hound's neck.

"I have it," he yelled.

One of the other fey had already turned and was trying to grab hold of the beast as well. Its short black fur didn't glint in the red light, but its teeth did. The hound shook its head, tearing into Ghua's flesh further. Terrified for Ghua and the rest of us, a sound escaped me. The hound's attention shifted, its glowing eyes pinning me.

It released its hold on Ghua and tensed, readying itself to jump over him. Another of the fey thrust a spear through its side. It didn't yip or anything. As if time slowed, I watched the thing start to spring upward. The fey with the spear pushed harder, the veins in his face bulging with his effort until his spear erupted from the hound's other side. Yet another leapt forward, closing his hands around the bloodied shaft, the two fey abruptly stopping the hound's upward progress.

Ghua turned and ran toward me.

He pushed me against the wall, caging me in with his body. The sound of growls and splintering wood filled the air. I looked up at Ghua, terrified. That hound wanted me, and we both knew it. Ghua's calm gaze met my frightened one.

"Nothing on this Earth will hurt you so long as I live," he said. "I love you, my Eden."

Something crashed into him, and he grunted but stayed protectively around me. Each jostle from behind made his face twist with pain until he closed his eyes against it. I'd seen what the hounds could do, the infected that shambled around with missing parts because they'd been half eaten.

I knew what the hellhound was doing to Ghua. My tears fell freely as his grey skin began to pale.

"We almost have it, Ghua," one of the fey yelled.

The chaotic noise of the ongoing fight, the screams of the other humans, the howls of the hounds and the yelling fey, all faded into the background as I stared up at Ghua. I placed my hand on his chest.

"I'll stay with you if you promise to stay with me," I said.

Ghua didn't answer.

"Got it," a voice said a moment later.

The jostling from behind Ghua stopped, and he stilled. In the sudden hush that dominated the bunker, I listened to his panting breaths and reached up to cup his face. He hadn't yet opened his eyes.

"Are you okay?"

His knees gave out, and he slowly started to crumble to the floor. I grabbed at his good arm, too afraid of hurting him more, but my hold didn't stop his fall. Kerr shook a handful of black dust from his hand and grabbed me before I could crouch down beside Ghua.

"No, Eden," Kerr said, grabbing my arm to stop me. "He can't be infected by the hound's saliva, but you can. Avoid all the blood."

I looked down at Ghua's exposed back. The hound had used its claws, ravaging the grey skin with deep furrows. Holes the size of the hound's teeth also marred the expanse. Blood ran from the open wounds. I grabbed a clean hand towel and handed it to Kerr. He took the towel from my hand and applied pressure to Ghua's back.

I looked up numbly at Molev, who strode into the room. Like many of the fey, he bore signs of the struggle with the hound. Their leader moved toward Ghua and inspected the wounds.

"The bleeding is slowing. Ghua will live, Eden. I promise you."

"What happened?" I asked. "How did the hellhounds even get in?"

"One of the humans opened the door for them."

"What?"

He tilted his head in the direction of the main corridor, and I followed him out there. The fey in the cramped space had suffered from the attack. So many wounded sat leaning against the wall. But, none of these fey were hurt as badly as Ghua. However, it was a different story for the human who sat among them. Ty. As I watched, he vomited and held his stomach.

Molev wouldn't let me move any closer.

"He will turn soon," he said.

"What happens then?"

"We will remove his head."

A soft murmur of voices drew my attention to the cage where another group of fey surrounded a man who lay on the floor. The man's lifeless eyes and blood coated middle told me he had died fighting.

One of the fey surrounding him, bent down and pressed his

forehead to the dead man's.

"In this life to the next, I will remember you, brother."

As the fey stood, Ty groaned in pain. With anger in his eyes, a fey walked to Ty and removed his head. None of the fey reacted, and I was the only human present. The act shocked me, but not because it had been Ty and he hadn't turned yet. More because it had been disgustingly wet sounding with some crunching.

"Mya will not like that he was killed before he turned," Molev said, studying me.

"I'm sure not going to tell her. But, if she happens to find out, I'll be sure to let her know he wasn't worth her consideration."

He nodded his thanks and led me to the room with all the survivors.

The wall of fey clogging the entrance to the bunk room parted to let us through. Oscar stood at the end of the fey passage, his arms crossed and his face red as he glared at us. Further into the room, the workers huddled together.

"It's okay," I said. "The hellhound is dead."

"Both of them," Molev said.

"We're lucky we're not dead," Oscar said. "These idiots wouldn't give us our weapons when the attack started."

"Good. Unless you wanted to be dead like Ty, who, by the way, opened the door to let the hellhounds in. You wouldn't know anything about that, would you?"

Oscar uncrossed his arms and stared at me.

"That's what I thought." My gaze shifted to the clock on the wall. "Four more hours until dawn, then we'll be out of your hair."

I turned and went back to the kitchen where Kerr and

another fey were lifting Ghua.

“Should you be moving him?” I asked, hurrying toward them. Ghua’s eyes weren’t open yet. My stomach twisted and churned with worry.

“He won’t be able to run and will be more comfortable traveling with Nancy’s children in the back of the truck. To keep them, and you, safe, we need to wash off the hound’s saliva.”

I watched them leave the room then sat heavily at the table. It would do no good to follow them. Not only would Kerr likely warn me away again, I also knew how cramped the bathroom would be with three people.

Once they had Ghua clean, they brought him to one of the beds in the bunk room. I sat beside him and waited for him to wake up. He didn’t, and the hours till dawn stretched endlessly.

Nineteen

The truck's bouncing progress slowed to a stop. Ghua, who lay on his stomach, didn't move. Just like he hadn't moved when the other fey had carried him out of the bunker. I tried not to think what that might mean, but the hard ball of fear hadn't left my stomach since he'd fallen to his knees.

While Ghua remained motionless, the survivors crowded into the space with us didn't. Those near the back tried to look through the canvas covered mesh gate.

As I'd guessed, every single one of the workers chose to leave the bunker. The unexpected twist came from Oscar, who'd asked if there was room for his group of men to go with us. Before I had a chance to laugh, Will had told Oscar, in no uncertain terms, that he and his men wouldn't be welcomed at Whiteman. The family-oriented camp needed people who were willing to work together to build a better future, not people who wanted to enslave the weak.

Oscar's parting words still rang in my ears.

"We need workers."

I could only hope that the fey would find any survivors in that area before Oscar's men could. Like Ghua had found and saved me.

I reached out and smoothed my hand over Ghua's hair, hoping he'd feel it and wake up. He didn't, though, and I struggled not to cry. It wasn't enough to have Molev say Ghua would be all right. I needed to hear it from Ghua's lips.

The canvas on the back of the truck opened, and light poured in. It hadn't taken us nearly as long to return to Whiteman because of the roads the fey had cleared on the way to the bunker.

I blinked, my eyes adjusting to see the fey leader. While the rest of the passengers were too caught up in their own troubles to notice mine, Molev's steady gaze hadn't missed a thing.

"Go," he said to someone off to the side of the truck before addressing me.

"We are here. We must take him inside, Eden," he said.

I nodded. He and Kerr climbed into the truck. With Molev at Ghua's head and Kerr at his feet, they carefully turned Ghua to his side. I wanted them to hurry and get him to wherever he needed to go for help. They moved slowly though, picking him up and easing him from the truck.

Ghua groaned once they were out, the first sound he'd made since the hound attack.

"All is well," Molev assured, looking up at me. "Feeling pain means he will live."

I jumped out of the back to follow them through the survivors congregated around the truck. The truck's door banged closed, and I looked back to see Will hurrying our way. He didn't say anything as he walked beside me.

Molev and Kerr moved steadily toward the white building and had almost made it to the door when it opened. Matt Davis strode out. He took in Ghua's condition and the survivors behind us in a single glance then moved to hold the door open.

"What happened?"

"We freed the humans who were being held," Molev said.

"One of the humans didn't like our interference and let two hellhounds in the bunker."

"It's true," Will said, as if Matt wouldn't have believed Molev without verification. "One of the men holding the survivors prisoner opened the hatch."

Molev and Kerr cleared the door and started across the large open space to a screened-in area toward the back.

"The hounds were drawn to the humans. Ghua was protecting Eden."

My eyes started to water, and I had to look away.

"Where is the woman who heals you?" Molev asked.

We rounded the screen area, and I saw several beds with clean, white sheets and shelves of supplies.

"I don't think there's much we can do for him," Matt said, studying Ghua's back. "Are you sure he's still alive?"

"He is alive," Molev said. "Where is the woman?"

"Will, please find Mrs. Feld."

Will nodded and ran from the area. The heavy fall of his footsteps echoed in the building until the door slammed closed.

"I am truly grateful for the help you've given us and for bringing the survivors here," Matt said in the sudden silence.

"We did not bring all of them. The men who took the children were left behind," Molev said.

"Will said they wouldn't be welcome here," I clarified so Matt wouldn't think it was Molev's decision to leave anyone behind. "They aren't good people. He made a good call."

"Yes. He and I talked before you set out. I trusted him to evaluate the situation and speak on my behalf and on behalf of every person here."

"You know leaving them behind doesn't fix the problem. They'll look for more people."

"And we'll visit them again," Matt promised.

I glanced at Ghua, wondering if it was worth the price. To Matt, who wasn't risking anything, who was gaining more able-bodied people at Whiteman, it was undoubtedly worth the price. But what about for the fey?

"One of the fey died there." I looked at Matt. "They carried him from the bunker until the first lake."

"We returned him to the water, but he will live on in our minds," Kerr said.

"By leaving those men behind, you've created a need to go back and risk losing another fey or two because we both know you can't check on them without the fey's help."

"I thought you said it was a good call to leave them behind."

"No. I said it was a good call not to bring them here. It would have been a better call to just kill them on the spot."

"We can't start acting as executioners," Matt said.

"Why not? They did. They killed Nancy's husband in the street when he tried to stop them from taking his kids."

"We have laws. Trials to prove innocence or guilt."

"In the old world. In the new world, hesitating or making the wrong choices will get innocent people killed."

The door opened, and two sets of hurried footsteps came our way.

Will rounded the corner with a woman. She didn't look old enough to be a doctor. I guessed she was in her early twenties, maybe. Not a single white strand interrupted the fall of her dark hair. Her red-rimmed eyes swept over us before landing on Ghua. I didn't miss the way her steps slowed for a moment before she regained her purposeful walk.

"Will said you needed me?" She kept her gaze fixed on Matt as she spoke.

"Yes. We need you to clean the fey's wounds. Please."

"His name is Ghua," I said. Her gaze flicked to me before returning to Matt.

"After the last breach, we have very few supplies left. We've already emptied the base's clinic. I'm not sure we have enough supplies to clean and suture the wounds."

"How do you know? You've barely looked at him," I said.

The door opened again, but I didn't pay attention to who was joining our little party.

"He's covered with lacerations from the back of his head to his thighs. I don't need to count them to know it's a lot."

Matt looked at Molev. "How quickly will he heal on his own?"

"Are you serious?" I said. "Get your damn supplies out and fix him. I don't care if you run out. The fey can find more."

Molev grunted in agreement.

"They aren't easy to come by," Matt said. "Clinics and hospitals are usually within cities. If they haven't been bombed, they're overrun with infected."

Two people rounded the screen. It took a moment to recognize Mya with her windblown hair. Drav nodded to Molev then went to Ghua. He bent and started speaking so softly in his ear that I couldn't hear what he was saying. I doubted it mattered as much as what Mya had to say, though.

"This is exactly what I'm talking about," she said, her hands on her hips. "If it were a human on that table, you wouldn't even hesitate to use the supplies if it meant saving a life. If you really want to save human lives, you do everything you can to keep the fey alive. Because if they die, we die. When are you going to get that through your heads?

"How many of you would have starved already if not for the

supply runs they do? How many more would be dead if the fey weren't here to help fight off the infected? Think long and hard about where you would be without them before you decide their lives have less value than anyone else's."

Matt looked at the nurse.

"Use what we have." He focused on Mya. "You're wrong. I wouldn't have wanted to use the sutures on a human hurt this badly, either. It would have been a waste because the weak tend to die here. But as you've pointed out, the fey are not weak."

Mya crossed her arms, looking stubbornly unforgiving.

Mrs. Feld moved to the shelves and started grabbing supplies.

I watched as she began cleaning the wounds to prepare for all the stitches she'd need to place. She didn't talk much as she worked. Matt and Molev quietly left the area, with Mya and Drav not far behind. Kerr stayed with me and watched Mrs. Feld work. I paced and chewed at the skin around my fingers, something I hadn't done since freshman year in high school.

"How long will he need the stitches in?" I asked when she opened the last pack.

"I'm honestly not sure. I think maybe seven days."

"Do they heal faster?"

"I don't know." She glanced at Kerr then quickly away. "I'm not a doctor, and none of the fey have needed my help before."

"We do heal faster," Kerr said. "Not as fast as when we're in the caves, but faster than humans seem to."

The woman ducked her head and made a sniffling sound. When she moved to wipe her face with the back of her hand, Kerr stopped her.

"He was bitten by a hound. It would be safer if you did not put his blood on your face."

She nodded and tied off the last stitch. I moved closer to Ghua as she started to clean up all the suture wrappers. She tossed everything, along with the gloves, into the trash then went to wash her hands in the nearby sink. When I caught her reflection in the mirror, I saw her tears.

A lot of people cried nowadays. Fear, frustration, and grief were a normal part of life now. But, not for me. Not anymore. I carefully held Ghua's hand.

Mrs. Feld came back over.

"That's all I can do," she said. "I don't know if I've actually helped him or not, but I did my best."

She'd stitched the deepest gashes first, then used what materials she had left to work on the wounds Ghua would be more likely to reopen if no stitches were in place. Between the stitches, butterfly bandages, and wrapped gauze, Ghua looked a bit like a mummy now. But a breathing mummy.

"What's your name?" I asked, noting her eyes were dry once more.

"Cassie."

"Thank you for helping him, Cassie."

She nodded and walked away. Kerr watched her leave. I watched Ghua breathe. His chest expanded and contracted in a steady rhythm. That had to be a good sign. At least, that's what I kept telling myself.

Not even a full 24 hours had passed since the attack. Yet, it felt like I'd been waiting for Ghua to wake up for days. I pulled a chair close to the bed and sat there, holding his hand.

* * * *

"Eden."

Ghua's voice penetrated my dream, and it took a few moments to realize I'd fallen asleep in the chair. Yawning, I sat up straight and opened my eyes. The light had faded in the building, and Kerr was nowhere around.

I looked at Ghua and found him watching me.

"Ghua! I thought I'd dreamt you saying my name. Are you okay? Do you need something to drink?"

"A drink would be good."

I went to the sink and grabbed one of the paper cups from the nearby shelf. When I got it back to him, I hesitated.

"Maybe I can find a straw."

"No. I can drink."

He accepted the cup and lifted himself up enough to gulp down the water before settling on his stomach again.

I took the empty cup from his hand and started playing with it as we studied one another.

"I thought you wouldn't wake up," I said softly.

He reached out for my hand. The warmth of his skin against mine brought tears to my eyes. I'd thought he would never touch me like this again.

"I was terrified you would die."

"I will never leave you."

I gave his hand a squeeze. He might believe his words, but I wasn't so sure.

"How do you feel? Your back looks like it belongs to Frankenstein."

"I look like more of a monster, now?"

"No. You don't look like a monster at all. Just really, really hurt."

He grunted.

"You're not going to tell me how much it hurts, are you?"

He grinned slightly.

"It hurts less when you're touching me."

I pulled my chair close and lightly traced my fingers over his face. He closed his eyes with a sigh. Soon his breathing evened out again.

"We'll leave at first light," a familiar voice said behind me.

I glanced toward the screened opening and saw Molev.

"Good. I think he'll be more comfortable at home."

Molev nodded and left. I didn't fall asleep, again. Instead, I kept touching Ghua's face, hoping it would be enough to bring him some comfort even in his sleep.

When the room began to brighten, I left his side to find a bathroom. I stared at myself in the mirror, not really seeing the dark circles under my eyes or my head of tangled, dark hair. What I saw was the fear in my eyes. This time it wasn't the infected or hellhounds that had put it there.

Everything that I'd faced, all the terror and the moments I'd thought would be my last, had nothing on what I'd felt until the moment Ghua had opened his eyes again. Yet, I still worried about what would come next. It wasn't really a choice anymore. I couldn't imagine staying behind at Whiteman. Yet, I knew what going with Ghua would mean. He already had my trust and my heart. Once I told him that, I knew what was next.

Dongzilla.

I shivered and ran the water to wash my face. While I cleaned up, I kept reminding myself I'd have time. He was hurt pretty badly.

When I returned to Ghua, I found him awake and standing and talking to Kerr.

"Are you sure you should be up?" I asked, hurrying toward him.

He wrapped his good arm around me and pulled me close. I leaned against his chest, careful not to touch anything bandaged.

He smelled faintly of soap and antiseptic as I pressed my face to his skin.

"I am fine, Eden," he said, smoothing a hand over my hair and down my back. "It is easier for me to walk to the truck than to be carried."

"The sun is coming up," Kerr said. "We can leave as soon as Ghua limps his way outside."

I peered up at him, worried that just walking would rip something open. Ghua looked down at me, planted a kiss on my forehead, and grinned at Kerr.

"Go. My pain will be less with your absence."

Kerr laughed and walked away.

"Do you need help?" I asked.

He shook his head.

"But, you can walk in front of me to give me something to focus on."

I grinned, unable to help myself. The guy was probably in a shit ton of pain, and he wanted to stare at my ass.

"Fine. I'll walk slowly, though."

He gave me another kiss then swatted my butt lightly as I turned away.

I laughed and exaggerated my walk.

It took five minutes to get to the truck and another three for Ghua to crawl into the back on his hands and knees then lay on the blanket that had been placed there for him. Nancy and the kids rode in the back with us while an escort of fey ran beside us.

"I thought you'd stay at Whiteman," I said once we cleared the gates.

Nancy shook her head.

"I'm not stupid enough to let pride or discrimination influence my decisions. Fear is a different story. I've seen the way these guys fight. They killed two hounds. I want my kids to live where they will be the safest, and Molev said there'd be room for us at Tolerance."

"There is. But you know what they want, right?"

Nancy looked at her daughter. Brenna smiled and set her head against her mother's shoulder. Her gaze, similar in color to her mother's, met mine.

"I know what they'll want," Brenna said. "And I know, this time, I'll have a choice."

The way she said it made my stomach sink.

"I'm sorry we couldn't get there sooner."

"I'm alive and safe. Not many people can say that."

"You will be safe with us," Ghua said from his prone position on the floor. "And, if you do not want to have sex, just say you are twelve. That is what Eden does."

He said it all with complete seriousness, and I grinned at Brenna.

"They have a thing about kids. Until you're eighteen, you're off limits."

"No, Eden. Until you're ready, you're off limits."

I stared at the man, losing even more of my heart to him.

Twenty

The first day back was rough on Ghua. He spent most of his time lying on his stomach in bed. He didn't complain, but when he thought I wasn't looking, he'd move around, showing his discomfort.

The second day, he walked around the house. Standing up straight didn't seem to bother him at all. However, going up and down the stairs produced a few winces. Throughout the day, I kept him company wherever he went. If he wanted to lay on the bed, I laid beside him. And, we spent a lot of time talking. I asked him questions about his first few days on the surface. I couldn't imagine discovering a whole new world. He told me about the confusion he and the other men felt when seeing humans and then the curiosity once Drav discovered the first female, Mya. Most of it was fairly amusing because of his naivety. Some of it was sad like when they discovered what death meant here.

I snuggled close to Ghua's side and ran my fingers through his hair.

"I don't like this," he said.

I immediately stopped. "Sorry."

"Not your touch. I will always like that. I do not like waiting to heal. It takes too long."

I grinned and went back to petting his hair.

"Cassie said that if you were human, you would need to wait almost two weeks before getting some of these stitches out. Since you're different, she's not sure how long it will take. Molev said you heal quickly. So, be thankful it's not two weeks of this."

"I would not survive two weeks being unable to hold you."

I leaned forward and kissed his cheek.

"You're very strong. I think you would survive."

Smiling slightly, I closed my eyes and pretended not to hear his grumbling. I fell asleep to the weight of his good arm over my back.

When I woke first, I slipped from bed to use the bathroom and shower. The hot spray felt so good, I lingered. After returning, I'd been so preoccupied with Ghua that I hadn't really paid attention to much else. It would take time to get used to the idea that I had easy and safe access to regular bathing and clean clothes. Well, clean clothes if I was willing to walk around in one of his oversized shirts while mine washed.

I turned off the water and dried. The idea of clean clothes had me ignoring the pile of dirty ones on the floor and wrapping the towel around my torso.

Ghua still breathed softly when I opened the door. Instead of going to the dresser, which made noise when opening the drawers, I went to the other door in the room. The door I hadn't opened on my first night in the house. It had to lead to a walk-in closet. I held a tiny spark of hope that I'd find it stuffed with women's clothes, all my size. I was a dreamer like that. If I couldn't have that wish, I would settle for some board games.

As I turned the handle, I reconsidered those priorities. Board games would probably come in handier than clothes for me. Ghua needed something fun to do today.

I eased the door open and stepped into the large space.

Laundry baskets overflowing with a ridiculously extensive variety of dildos and vibrators filled the closet. Baskets were stacked on baskets. Some of them looked sorted based on the type of vibrator or dildo. Ghua had even set some individually on the shelves meant for shoes just inside the door. I stared at the black tinted rubber one that looked comparable in size to my forearm.

"Holy fu—"

"Eden! Do not go in there!" Ghua's panicked voice echoed in the room.

Reaching out an arm, I pushed the door wider so I could see him.

"I think you're a little late with the warning, buddy."

He started to move off the bed.

"You stay right where you are, Ghua, and start explaining why you have about a thousand fake penises in your closet. Because this shit is freaking me out. First porn magazines and now this?"

Not listening to me, he shifted himself off the bed. Then he stood there, looking around the room in that distressed way he had when I'd flashed him.

"Talk, Ghua. Why do you have all of these? Please tell me you haven't used them?"

"Me? No. They are for females."

"You weren't planning to use them on me, were you? Because I'm telling you now, that shit cannot be previously owned."

"No. I wasn't going to use them on anyone. I didn't know what they were for. Some of them looked very different from how my brothers and I look. I thought the human males weren't made like us and was curious about the differences. I thought it might help me understand why human females don't like us, so I started bringing them back from scavenging runs to study."

"This is not a sample. This is a collection."

"I will remove them."

"You bet you will. I can't believe you even kept this many. Please tell me you washed your hands after touching them."

"Why?"

"Because by touching them, you've touched a thousand vaginas!"

He smiled slightly.

"I like vagina."

"What?"

"It is a good word. Mya doesn't like us to use the word pussy. I will use vagina now."

"No you will not. Pussy and vagina aren't words used in normal conversation."

"We're using them now."

"This is not a normal conversation."

He sighed heavily. "Why do you and Mya not want to talk about the things we find most interesting?"

For a moment, I could only stare at him, dumbfounded.

"You need a hobby. Something to get your mind off of constantly thinking about sex."

"I do not think about sex all the time. But I do think about pussy and boobs a lot."

I covered my face with my hands, unable to believe Ghua's single track mind.

"Are you angry, Eden?" he asked softly.

I looked up at him and shook my head.

"Angry? No. Worried? Yes. I'm just not sure yet who I should be worried about more. You or me?"

"You do not need to worry about either of us."

"You know what? I'm going to put a shirt on and go wash my clothes. Let's pretend that I am mad at you, and you're smart enough to give me some space to cool off."

"You're angry and too warm?"

"You're making my brain hurt."

I closed the door on the freak fest in his closet and grabbed my clothes from the bathroom. Ghua was smart enough to stay in the bedroom and not try to follow me downstairs.

It gave me time to sort through what I was feeling. I wasn't angry. Not really. Weirded out a bit, definitely. But I couldn't really say his fascination with porn and sex toys was so unusual. Just about every boy I'd known had gone through that stage. Heck, some probably never left that phase of their life. Ghua was very much like a boy learning things about girls. It was all new and fascinating.

Feeling better about the situation, I left the laundry room and went back upstairs for a shirt.

Ghua was still by the bed. When he saw me, he scowled. The fierce expression stopped me in my tracks.

"Now you look like you're mad at me," I said.

"I am."

Surprisingly, that didn't worry me in the least.

"What did I do?"

He stalked across the room toward me.

"Did you mean what you said?"

"I said a lot already this morning. You're going to need to be more specific."

"Not this morning. When the hound was trying to get you, you said you would stay with me if I promised to stay with you." He reached out and hooked a finger in the front of my towel and tugged me close. "And, I stayed," he said. "I promise to always stay."

I stared up into his serious eyes.

"I don't understand why that is making you frown at me. I thought you wanted me to stay with you."

"I do."

"Then why are you mad?"

"Because you yelled at me and left. Because I'm tired of waiting for you to say you will stay. Because I want to touch you and hold you so much it hurts me here." He laid his free hand over his heart. "And it hurts more when you walk away."

I reached up and cupped his face.

"I will stay with you. If I get mad and need some space, it doesn't mean I've changed my mind, it just means I need some time to think things through."

He frowned again, and I pressed up on my tiptoes to kiss him lightly. When I pulled back, he studied me intently.

"Why don't you take a shower, and I'll make us some breakfast," I said. "Remember not to get the stitches wet."

"Will you help me?"

"I don't think that would be a smart choice this time."

"I think it would be."

"You'd end up hurting yourself, and it will take even longer to heal. Go. Shower. I'll be downstairs."

He grumped and stalked off to the bathroom. The water turned on as I changed into a clean shirt. Since he'd left the door open, I went in and hung my towel on a peg in the bathroom. Ghua looked at me through the glass half-wall. The heat in his gaze was unmistakable. He certainly did have one thing on his mind, and his injuries wouldn't hold him back forever.

"Remember not to let your stitches get wet."

He grunted.

I rolled my eyes and left the room.

I wished we had the ability to make a big breakfast. Waffles, pancakes, eggs and bacon, omelets...any of it would have been good. I settled for a bowl of cereal for me and a can of Spam for Ghua.

He came downstairs dressed in a pair of athletic shorts and ate his Spam in silence.

"Want to watch a movie or something today?" I asked. "I can angle the couch a little so you can see the TV while you're lying down."

"Yes."

He watched me nudge the couch into position then laid down with a sigh that said "my life sucks" while I put in a movie.

I'd barely settled in the recliner when he spoke up.

"My back itches."

"I think that's a good thing. It means it's healing."

"No, it means it itches. Can you scratch it?"

I went over by him and looked at the stitches and butterfly taped areas. The scabs over the wounds looked dark and thick but the skin around them completely normal. I gently scratched the non-broken areas as close to the injuries as I could.

He made an appreciative sound then lifted his head.

"I can't see. Sit here. You can scratch, and we can watch the movie."

"You're getting pretty bossy," I said, sliding in under him.

He set his head on my lap with another sigh. His exhales warmed the skin of my exposed thigh , reminding me I was only wearing a long t-shirt. The rest of my clothes continued to quietly swish in the washer down the hall. I really needed to figure out how to expand my wardrobe.

Ghua stretched his arm up, hooking it over my legs. I looked at the stitches and immediately felt bad. I was sitting there thinking about finding more underwear while he was trying to recover from helping save people.

He sighed again and rubbed his cheek against my lap as if he couldn't get comfortable. I continued to lightly scratch his skin.

"Do you want me to get you a pillow?"

His other arm snaked up behind me, cupping my hip.

"No. Don't leave."

I smiled slightly and focused on the movie.

We hadn't made it more than a few minutes in when I noticed Ghua breathing funny. His inhales were big and slow. His exhales were more shallow and quick.

"You okay?"

He turned his head slightly, as if rubbing an itch on his nose, then faced the TV again.

"I am okay."

"All right." I said it, but I didn't believe it because he shifted on the couch as if uncomfortable then made the same movement. This time, I noticed his chest expanding as he did it.

"Ghua, are you sniffing me?"

He stopped inhaling deeply.

"No."

"Are you having breathing problems, then?"

"No."

I stopped scratching his back and lightly played with his hair. My hand brushed his ear, and he groaned. His fingers dug into my thigh and hip, and he pulled me a little further under him. This time when he turned his head, there was no mistaking what he was doing.

"Ghua, it's not polite to sniff—"

He lifted his head and repositioned me before I knew what he intended. He had one of my legs wedged between his side and the back cushions, and the other leg dangled off the couch.

He laid his head on my lower stomach.

He could pretend to watch the movie all he wanted, but I wasn't stupid. I knew what he was up to. And against all common sense, I tingled with anticipation, and my pulse picked up speed.

His fingers stroked my backside through the shirt. Inch by inch, he worked the bottom of the shirt up my thigh, moving occasionally to free it from his weight.

The room grew warmer. Or maybe I did.

Struggling to keep my breathing even, I continued to play with his hair and stare at the screen. When he shifted again and his bare chest touched my pubic bone, I knew I was a goner.

"Ghua, I don't think this is a good idea."

He lifted his head to meet my gaze, then blatantly looked down at my exposed girl parts. I swallowed hard and forced myself to stay still. The last thing I wanted to do was rip a stitch while trying to wrestle my legs closed.

He lowered his head and inhaled deeply, proving that he had been sniffing me, then placed a kiss just inside my thigh.

"Do you trust me?"

"Yes."

He kissed the other thigh, his tongue flicking out to taste where his lips had been.

My hands forgot their purpose and idly stroked his ears instead of his hair. His breath escaped in a whoosh, heating my core. My chest tightened, and I played with his ears some more.

He groaned and looked up at me, his eyes full of intense emotion.

"Do you love me?"

There was no use trying to deny it anymore.

"Yes. I love you, Ghua."

He growled and ducked his head to nip at my thigh. Nibble by nibble, he worked his way to my center. He breathed deeply then his tongue swept over me in a long stroke. I gasped and involuntarily bucked my hips. His hands gripped my ass, and he pulled me closer. With his face pressed between my legs, he slowly explored each crease and swell. I panted and made noise each time he found a sweet spot.

He lifted his head, and I blinked down at him, dazed and aching for more.

"You are beautiful, my Eden. Your cheeks are pink and your lips wet. You love me and trust me. Will you allow me the rest?"

"Yes." The desperate answer escaped me before I could think of all the reasons why we shouldn't.

The moment he got off the couch and scooped me up into his arms brought clarity.

"Ghua, stop. You're going to hurt yourself."

He looked down at me and smiled.

"You shot me, and I still carried you. This is no different."

He started toward the stairs. Too afraid of hurting him, I didn't struggle in his arms.

"First, I'm really sorry I shot you. Second, you scolded me and said it hurt. So, I know this has to hurt, too."

"I hurt, but not because of the hound's scratches." He reached the top of the stairs and strode to the bedroom.

My pulse pounded as he placed me on the bed.

"Will you take your shirt off again?" he asked, hopeful.

Exhaling steadily, I reached down and pulled the shirt up and over my head. I tossed it aside and scooted further back to give him room. The king-sized bed gave plenty of that.

His gaze swept over me, then he grabbed the waistline of his shorts. I'd tried to ignore his erection until that point. However, once he freed it, I couldn't look away. Kicking the material to the side, he put a knee on the mattress.

"Please be careful," I said softly.

"I won't hurt either of us," he said crawling toward me.

I wasn't so sure about that.

When he reached me, he kissed my neck, nipping a trail down to my breast. He didn't need to coax me much to get me to lay back. While his tongue traced a slow circle around my nipple, his knee wedged between my legs. I arched up, wanting more.

"Please, Ghua."

His mouth closed over my tight bud, and I moaned at the hot, wet suction. The feel of his fingers, smoothing down the column of my throat, over my sternum, and down between my legs made me shiver with need. He stroked my folds, then shifted his attention to my mouth.

He kissed me reverently, pouring his tenderness into each touch of his tongue. He pulled back to look at me.

"I love you, Eden. You are brave and smart. You're patient and sometimes kind. I like that you're soft here," he traced his fingers over my breast, "and here," he slipped a finger inside of me.

The sweet man was trying to seduce me when he already had my legs spread wide.

I smiled at him and gently cupped his face.

"And I like that you're persistent and so very loyal."

He kissed me softly again and lifted himself. The head of his cock bumped my entrance. I tilted my hips and reached between us. My hand closed over him, and I wondered again if I was insane to say yes to this man.

He pushed forward, easing himself into my opening. Stretching me and pressing forward before withdrawing a bit. Inch by inch, he worked his way in, the advance and retreat slicking the way. Sweat beaded his brow by the time he was fully seated. I ached and burned but in a desperate, hot way that made it impossible for me to hold still. I arched up and swiveled my hips, grinding against him.

He growled and withdrew halfway. I groaned when he slowly pushed all the way in again with a single, slow stroke.

"More," I panted.

He withdrew and returned faster this time. Forgetting myself, I hooked my heel around the back of his leg. He reached back and gently removed it.

"Sorry," I whispered.

He kissed me hard then set a grueling pace that made me cry out and beg. He grunted in time with his thrusts, too. I'd never felt anything so amazing before in my life. As my insides tightened, I was already thinking of doing this again and again.

My climax exploded through me. I tensed and let out a low wail as Ghua kept thrusting. His rhythm faltered. He jerked inside of me twice, then roared. I could feel each pulse of his release.

He partially collapsed on top of me, his weight a comfort rather than a bother. His lips pressed against my forehead.

"That was amazing," I said.

He grunted and slipped to the side to lay on his stomach.

"Are you okay? Did I hurt you?"

"I have never felt better, my Eden. You've filled my heart so it will never ache again."

I smiled and rolled on my side. The heavy stickiness between my legs distracted me from what I'd been about to say.

"I think I need to shower," I said.

He immediately lifted his head.

"Can I help you?"

"Always."

Twenty-One

It took us three days to emerge from the house. Mostly because Ghua had refused to let me put any clothes on. He loved watching me walk around the house naked. I loved feeling safe enough to do so. I also loved the curtains.

"We will not stay out for long, Eden," Ghua said firmly, as I pulled the door closed behind us. "Humans get cold easily."

"Right. Because it's the cold you're worried about, not the lost time you could have spent playing with all my girl parts."

His stern expression turned wistful.

"I like your girl parts."

"And that's why we're doing this." I nodded toward the two bags he held, and the box I carried. "A girl wants to know she's not just a replacement sex toy." What we carried now was only a portion of the collection of porn and dildos he needed to get rid of, but it was a start.

He frowned at me.

"You are not a toy, Eden. If I could never touch you again, I would still beg you to stay with me. I love you because of what you do and say and think. Not because of your body or how you look."

I grinned.

"But you like how I look, too, don't you?"

That wistful expression returned.

"Oh, yes. Very much."

Knowing the direction of his thoughts, I laughed.

"Come on. Let's see where we can ditch this stuff before the sun sets."

We walked side by side toward the dump pile he'd told me about. I only hoped it was late enough in the afternoon that no one would be out to witness who was leaving Santa sized bags of dildos in the recycling heap.

"Molev!"

The yell echoed through the neighborhood, and the door of a house just down the street opened. I froze like a burglar in a spotlight.

"Ghua, we gotta go," I whispered.

I turned to dash back to our house but was brought up short at the sight of two men running toward us.

"Molev!" the one in the lead yelled again.

"Drav's going to get him," Mya called from behind us.

I looked over my shoulder and saw more people coming out of their houses and walking our way. There was no way to escape being seen, now.

Mya, Julie, and Mya's father hurried toward the two newcomers. Both fey looked in rough shape. Their clothes were dirty, their hair unwashed, and their skin covered with scrapes and scratches.

"Who are they?" I whispered to Ghua.

"Thallirin and Merdon. They are outcasts, exiled for killing Oelm." With an undecipherable expression, Ghua watched the two then glanced at me. "They said it was an accident."

"You don't believe them?"

The two groups met right in front of us. Afraid of drawing their attention, I stayed where I was. Ghua didn't leave my side.

"Looks like this hunt was rough," Mya said.

Thallirin nodded and held out three hearts.

"The hounds these belong to have been following us for days."

Merdon favored his right side slightly. I knew what kind of injury a hound could inflict and wondered just how badly he was injured.

Molev and Drav came around the corner with Nancy and her kids in tow. Everyone stopped talking and watched their approach. Around us, the lights imbedded into the wall came on one by one, dispelling the encroaching shadows.

"I'm here, Thallirin. Do it now so you can leave again," Molev said, coming to a stop beside Mya.

Thallirin lifted one of the dark, ragged rocks in his arms. It pulsed with negative light, a blackness that cast a shadow on anything around it.

He fitted his hand around the object and squeezed, his muscles bulging. I could hear the grinding crackles a moment before the thing disintegrated into black dust. He shook out his hand in a move reminiscent to what Kerr had done in the bunker.

Nancy wheeled toward us so she had a better view. Her kids followed. Thallirin glanced our direction as he gripped the second one.

Hoping what he did would be enough to distract any curiosity from the objects trying to stab through the sides of the semi-translucent bag Ghua held, I shifted the weight of the box in my arms and tried to be patient.

"That is eight, total," Molev said. "Go."

"Can't they at least stay the night?" Mya asked.

"It looks like Merdon could use some rest," Julie added.

"They struck a bargain. Ten hearts each for the life they

took."

Merdon swayed on his feet but bowed his head in acknowledgement and turned to go back the way he'd come.

"I know I'm new here," I said, hating myself for speaking up. "But it seems to me, for a people who live in a town named Tolerance and who've been mistreated by humans, you're pretty short on kindness to your own people."

"They are being punished and need to earn their place here."

"That's fine, but do you really want them to die in the process? Mya said that each fey matters. How will periods of rest negatively impact their punishment? Or better yet, how will losing two more of your brothers impact the future of our world?"

Merdon and Molev both watched me intently as I spoke. Thallirin, however, only had eyes for Brenna. The girl was pointedly ignoring the attention.

"Can I help you with that?" Brenna asked, reaching for the box I held and drawing everyone's attention to the fact Ghua and I had our arms full.

Mya's gaze flicked to the bags. Her eyes widened in recognition, and her gaze flew to me.

"Hey, I just got here a few days ago. This isn't from me," I said quickly.

No way was I getting the reputation as a pervert after only living here for such a short time. Hell, I didn't want that reputation ever. Not with this crowd.

She looked at Ghua. "Why would you collect these? Do you even know what they are?"

"Yes. Mom explained them to me."

"What?" Mya turned her shocked face toward her mother.

"Don't you give me that angry look, young lady. I answered the same questions for you and Ryan."

"No you didn't! I was smart enough not to ask them."

Julie chuckled.

"What are they?" Thallirin asked.

Mya opened her mouth to answer, but Ghua beat her to it.

"They are supposed to be like human man parts, but Eden says they are not. Human penises are not this big. Mine is extra-large."

Julie covered her mouth with a hand. Even Mya's dad grinned at Ghua. I, however, wanted to find a hole to crawl into.

"I think that's enough education time," Mya said briskly. "Mom, can you and Dad take Thallirin and Merdon to an empty house?"

"Of course."

"Try not to give them a full health class on the way there."

Julie laughed and shook her head at her daughter. The pair walked off with Mya's parents but not before Thallirin got one last look at Brenna.

"Maybe you should go with them," Mya said to Drav. He kissed her forehead then jogged to catch up with Mya's parents and the two new fey.

"I will walk you home," Molev said to Nancy.

Mya said nothing as they left. Ghua shifted uncomfortably under her scrutiny and glanced at me.

"Are you angry, Eden? Your face is red."

I sighed. "I'm not angry. I'm embarrassed."

"Welcome to my world," Mya said. "I'm sorry he managed to sneak those in. I've been trying to help them understand some things aren't appropriate."

"It's not your fault. It's his. He knew he wasn't supposed to have them because he hid them under the couch cushions and in his closet."

Mya groaned and shook her head at Ghua.

"You're very lucky that Eden's not too afraid of things. Seeing that many–"

"Man parts," Ghua supplied helpfully.

"Yes. Seeing that many could have sent her running for the hills, and you would have missed out on having a relationship of your own."

"This isn't even a quarter of what he has," I said.

"Seriously?"

"Very."

"What the hell are we going to do with all of them?"

"I was going to ditch them by the recycling pile."

"Hell no! That'll be like a free for all." She looked into the shadows around us. That's when I noticed we weren't really alone. Fey idled about, listening to our conversation.

"I changed my mind," I said. "I'm so mad at you, Ghua." I did not want to be stuck with his dildo collection.

He dropped his bags, scooped me up into his arms, and started back toward our house. I gripped the box I still held and stared up at Ghua in confusion.

"Hey," Mya called. "Where are you going?"

"I need to go play with Eden's girl parts to make her happy."

"Ghua!" I buried my face in his shoulder. "I can't believe you just said that loud enough for everyone to hear."

Mya laughed behind us.

"Don't worry, Eden. I'll take care of this and come get you tomorrow."

"Not before eight," Ghua called back. "Eden likes—"

I slapped my hand over his mouth.

"If you say it, we won't do it."

He leaned in and set his forehead against mine. I removed my hand.

"Yes, we will do it. Because you love my touch and what I say and what I do. You love me, my Eden. And I love you."

I tipped my head forward and pressed my lips to his in what was meant to be a quick kiss but turned out to be a toe curler.

"Take me home, you sweet man."

Epilogue

I covered my mouth and nose with a scarf and stared at the multicolored flames.

"Who knew burning dicks would smell so bad?" Mya said.

She stood by me with an empty can of gasoline.

"Let's just hope they don't melt into something worse."

"What could be worse than a mountain of dildos?"

"One giant one."

She laughed.

"Have those guys from last night left yet?" I asked.

"No. Merdon's hurt badly enough that one of the fey just left to go get Mrs. Felds."

"What's she going to do? She used all the supplies for stitches on Ghua."

"Kerr and a few others went out to go find more. He said he was watching what she was doing and thinks he knows what to get."

"Good."

"Thanks for sticking up for those two last night," she said.

"I had to. This world is a scary place, and you were right to point out that we'll need each one of them to survive it."

Mya nodded seriously for a moment then grinned.

"Not only do they keep us safe, they keep things entertaining, too. Do you know what I heard Ghua telling

Merdon this morning?"

I cringed, already knowing I wouldn't like it. "What?"

"The best distraction from the pain is playing with girl parts."

We both burst out laughing.

I had no regrets about the choices I'd made to get to where I was. Ghua was the best thing that could have happened to me. Sure, we'd had some bumps along the way, and he would likely continue to embarrass me, but I couldn't be happier. I would keep taking each perfect moment for my own in this imperfect world. And, I hoped I would grab enough that Ghua and I could build an amazing lifetime together here in Tolerance, surrounded by our family.

Author's Note

Thank you for reading! Becca and I loved writing the initial Demon trilogy together. However, our schedules didn't quite mesh for continuing with more books. Hopefully, you didn't notice too much of a difference. ☺

Your support keeps me writing! Please tell other readers about these books, or leave a review to spread the word about a story you loved or hated. Books with more reviews have increased visibility on retailer sites, so each review counts! And don't forget to watch for Demon Deception, the next book in the Resurrection Chronicles.

If you want to keep up to date on my release news, teasers, and special giveaways, please consider subscribing to my newsletters. mjhaag.melissahaag.com/subscribe (I only send periodically, so you won't be overwhelmed.)

Until next time!

Melissa

Also by M.J. Haag

Beastly Tales

Depravity

Deceit

Devastation

Lutha Chronicles

Escaping the Lutha

Facing the Lutha

Resurrection Chronicles

Demon Ember

Demon Flames

Demon Ash

Connect with the author

Website: MJHaag.MelissaHaag.com

Newsletter: MJHaag.MelissaHaag.com/subscribe

Made in the USA
Lexington, KY
26 October 2018